# "Got you at lasssst. . . ."

Four torches, mounted on poles, formed a square around me. I heard an evil chuckle to my right. I turned toward it, and the flickering light provided my first sight of the creature who had dragged me here. He was foul looking, with long hair that hung around his shoulders in greasy strings. When he beckoned to me, I saw that he had long, yellowed fingernails; when he smiled, he showed sharp, rotting teeth. His eyes glittered with malice from their deep sockets. Yet for all that, I could tell that he had once been human, which may have been the scariest thing of all.

That, and the fact that he looked oddly familiar. With a shudder, I realized I had seen him in my dreams—or, to be more accurate, in my nightmares.

"Got you at lasssst," he said in a hissing voice that was filled with deep satisfaction. "Got you at lasssst."

**Other Bruce Coville anthologies from Scholastic include:**

*Bruce Coville's Book of Monsters*
*Bruce Coville's Book of Aliens*
*Bruce Coville's Book of Ghosts*

# BRUCE COVILLE'S
# BOOK OF

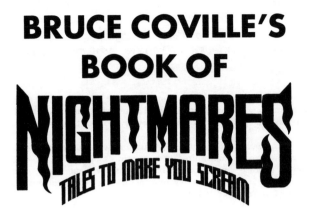

**NIGHTMARES**
**TALES TO MAKE YOU SCREAM**

Compiled and edited by
Bruce Coville

Illustrated by
John Pierard

A GLC Book

AN
**APPLE**
PAPERBACK

SCHOLASTIC INC.
New York Toronto London Auckland Sydney

*For Peter Lerangis,
despite the fact that he never sent me a story.*

No part of this publication may be reproduced in whole or in part, or stored in a retrieval system, or transmitted in any form or by any means, electronic, mechanical, photocopying, recording, or otherwise, without written permission of the publisher. For information regarding permission, write Scholastic Inc., 555 Broadway, New York, NY 10012.

ISBN: 0-590-46161-3

10  9  8  7  6  5  4  `                    6  7  8  9/9  0/0

Printed in the U.S.A.                                    40

First Scholastic printing February 1995

# CONTENTS

# Contents

# INTRODUCTION:
# DON'T READ THIS BOOK!

That title is no joke. You probably shouldn't read this book. Certainly not if you get scared easily, are subject to night frights, or don't like being spooked out. After all, I take my titles seriously, and there are stories in this book that I think are genuine nightmare material. (Just ask the poor editor who had to work on the manuscript with me!)

But look at this: You're still reading!

I bet you're going to ignore my warning altogether, aren't you?

Well, it doesn't surprise me. For some reason, most people seem to like being scared.

In fact, I would even say that people *need* to be scared every once in a while. I think it's built right into us, bone deep. After all, fear has been part of our lives for millions of years now.

# Introduction

It is only in the recent past (when you think in terms of the human species) that most people have been able to lead a relatively safe life. For the bulk of the time that humans have existed, survival has meant being able to run or fight at an instant's notice. And, of course, those who could find a sudden burst of speed or surge of strength were the ones most likely to survive and have children.

Our bodies have developed a special chemical that provides that speed and strength. It's called adrenaline, and a sudden squirt of it not only sets your heart racing, it can, in extreme situations, let you do things that normally would be simply impossible.

The thing is, once you set up a system like that, it has to be used now and then. (Just as the fire alarms in your school have to be tested every once in a while.) Which means that some part of our mind keeps looking to be scared— if only to test the system!

At least, that's what I think.

I'll give you an example from my own life. When I was twenty, I worked at a summer camp that was located at the end of a bumpy dirt road that wound for eighteen miles through a deserted forest. This road was closely edged by gnarled old trees; in places their branches linked overhead to form a strange roof. At night, it was extraordinarily spooky.

When my wife and I had made a trip to town and were driving back to camp along this road after dark, we often tried to scare each other by playing "What if?"

"What if," she would ask me, "a strange-looking old woman dressed in black came out of the woods and waved to us to stop? Would you do it?"

"What if I did stop, and she climbed onto the car and started pounding on the windshield?" I would reply. "What if she was screaming 'Let me in, let me in!' What would you do?"

Before long, we would have ourselves so scared we couldn't think straight.

But that didn't stop us from playing the game. Something about the human heart loves a good scare—especially if you know at the same time that you are actually safe.

The thing is, we're never *really* safe from that scare. Because even when we know something is impossible, our minds persist in making us believe that the unreal can be real, that the darkness under the bed is solid and coming to get us, that fear and death and terror are waiting in the night.

Well, since terror lurks at the edges of

our minds, we might as well make friends with it.

So, go ahead—read this book.

But if you can't sleep tonight—don't blame me.

After all, I did warn you.

Heh heh heh.

# SPECIAL NOTE

In *Bruce Coville's Book of Monsters*, the first book in this series, we announced a scary story contest, with the winner to be published in this volume. Our readers didn't let us down. We got a *flood* of stories—over 2,000 in all!

I don't think it is any insult to the winning story for me to tell you that it was very difficult to make my final choice from that sea of stories: I had a *lot* of great tales to choose from. I finally settled on Steven Prohaska's deliciously spooky "Halloween Party" because in addition to its strong, vivid writing, it was exactly the kind of story I wanted to read myself when I was a kid (which is one of the ways I judge my own books when I am working on them).

Like all the other writers in this volume, Steve worked with me on editing his story. He was an editor's dream: polite, prompt, and creative. I hope he chooses to continue writing, because I think he has a great future ahead of him.

The good news is, so do many of the rest of you.

Thanks for all your terrific stories.

*I like to write in the first person—that is,*
*as if I actually am the person telling the story.*
*One problem with this style is that it can*
*sometimes reduce suspense. After all, if*
*someone is telling a story, you can be*
*pretty sure that he or she lived through it.*
*Of course, living through something doesn't*
*mean you haven't come out* different
*on the other side. . . .*

# THERE'S NOTHING UNDER THE BED

## Bruce Coville

I suppose I can't really blame my parents for not believing me when I told them about the weirdness under my bed. After all, adults never believe a kid when he or she talks about that kind of thing. Oh, they'll believe you're *afraid,* of course. But they never believe you've actually got a good reason to feel that way. They'll certainly never believe you if you tell them something horrible is lurking under the bed, waiting to take you away.

But you and I know they should. You and I know that there *are* terrible things that hide there, waiting to catch you, snatch you, steal you.

At least, I know. Because now I'm one of them.

I'm not sure when I first realized there was something wrong under my bed. I must have been fairly young, because I can remember one night when I was about five or six I rolled a ball under the bed by accident. I heard a popping sound and started to cry because I knew I would never get my ball back from the weird gray nothingness down there.

So clearly I knew about the nothingness by then and understood that things disappeared into it. But at the time I was upset simply because I had lost my ball. Like a kid who needs glasses but doesn't know it, and just assumes things look fuzzy to everyone else, too, I figured this was the way the world was.

Besides, everyone loses things in their bedroom—socks, pencils, yo-yos, homework you're certain you did. It wasn't until I began staying overnight at my friends' houses and saw the incredible messes under their beds—messes that *didn't disappear*—that I realized something was truly wrong at my house.

My second clue came when I tried to tell

my parents about this and they thought I was playing a silly game. "For heaven's sake, David," said my mother. "Don't be ridiculous!"

I remember these words well, because I heard them so many times in the months that followed. The few times I actually did manage to drag Mom and Dad up to look under my bed, the weird gray nothingness wasn't there and all they saw was solid floor. That happened sometimes. Finally I realized that the nothingness disappeared whenever grown-ups were around. As you can imagine, this was very frustrating.

After a while Mom and Dad decided to get me some "special help"—which is to say, they sent me to a shrink. Unfortunately the nothingness under my bed wasn't something that could be fixed by a shrink. All I learned from the experience was that I had better keep my mouth shut if I didn't want to get sent away for even more intense treatment.

Personally, I think Mom should have figured out that a kid as sloppy as I was could never naturally have a bed that didn't even have dust bunnies under it! But Weztix has taught me that people will believe really stupid things in order to avoid having to believe something they think is impossible. I guess Mom just assumed that my losing so much stuff simply indicated I was even lazier, sloppier, or more addlebrained than most kids.

Maybe I was. That didn't mean that the area under my bed wasn't weird and scary.

Even so, I managed to live with it—until the day it swallowed Fluffy.

Yeah, I know: "Fluffy" is a disgustingly cute name for a cat. But when we got Fluffy she was a disgustingly cute kitten. And according to my parents I was a disgustingly cute toddler. So when I wanted to call the kitten Fluffy, they were happy to oblige.

As you get older, you discover certain things you wish your parents had done differently, maybe even been a little stricter about. Naming our cat Fluffy was one of them. By fifth grade I had earned at least two black eyes from fights that started with people teasing me about my "sissy cat."

Not that Fluffy cared what anyone called her, as long as we fed her on time. She was pretty aloof. But she was mine, and I loved her.

Fortunately, Fluffy seemed to have figured out on her own that she should avoid the area under my bed. Maybe it was some instinctive awareness of danger. Whatever the reason, I never had to worry about losing her there. She just naturally avoided the area.

If it hadn't been for my rotten cousin Harold, I doubt she would ever have gone under there.

When I was little and got upset my mother used to say, "Well, David, into every life a little rain must fall."

If that's true, then Harold was my own personal thunderstorm. Two years older than me and about forty pounds of solid muscle heavier, Harold projected all the friendly charm of a porcupine having a bad hair day.

Even so, his mother adored him—a fact probably worth a scientific study all by itself.

Harold and his mother came to visit more often than I would have liked. Well, once in a hundred years was really more often than I would have liked, but Harold and Aunt Marguerite actually showed up almost once a month—including the day that I was stolen.

I had already had a rough week, and when I found out that they were coming that day, I threw myself to the floor and screamed, *"Just kill me now and get it over with!"*

"That's not funny, David," said my mother.

"I'm not trying to be funny," I replied.

They came anyway.

As usual, Aunt Marguerite had "private things" to discuss with my mother—meaning that she was having trouble with her latest boyfriend and wanted Mom's advice. In my opinion, Aunt Marguerite's endless string of boyfriends was one source of Harold's problems. But no one asked me. Anyway, the fact that she wanted to talk to Mom meant that I got to entertain Harold.

It was a wretched, rainy day, so the two of us had to play up in my room. After a while Harold grabbed Fluffy and said, "How about a game of Kitty Elephant?"

Kitty Elephant is something Harold invented, and it will tell you a lot about him. Basically it consists of putting a sock over a cat's face so that it looks like it has a long trunk, then laughing hysterically while you watch the cat try to get out of it.

I had learned to stay out of the way when Harold was doing something rotten, but when I saw Fluffy getting too close to the bed I tried to grab her. Harold grabbed me first. Twisting my arm behind my back, he hissed, "Don't interfere with the game, Beanbrain."

"Harold, you don't understand!"

"I understand that you're a wuss," he said. "I'm embarrassed to have you for a cousin."

I thought about telling him that I was *disgusted* to have him as a cousin, but decided against it, since he had already twisted my arm so far behind my back it felt like it was coming out of its socket.

Fluffy was getting closer to the edge of the bed.

"Let me *GO!*" I screamed.

To my surprise, Harold did let go—mostly, I think, to keep our mothers from coming up to see what was going on. It was too late. In her efforts to get the sock off her head, Fluffy had rolled under the bed.

A bolt of lightning sizzled through the rainy sky.

For an instant I had dared to hope that this was one of the times when the floor was in its solid state. The lightning told me that it was not. And when I heard a *pop*, like someone pulling their finger out of a bottle, I knew Fluffy was gone.

The popping sound drew Harold to the edge of the bed. "Come on out, Fluffy," he said, reaching under to grab her.

When he couldn't find her, he bent and lifted the edge of the bedspread. Then he scrambled over the bed and looked down the other side.

"What happened?" he asked nervously. "Where did she go?"

"Why don't you crawl under there and find out?" I said bitterly, feeling so wretched I thought I might throw up.

Having Harold as a witness did not, of

course, mean that our mothers were going to believe us. Nor did it help matters that when we finally did convince Mom and Aunt Marguerite to come upstairs we found Fluffy sitting on my bed, licking her paws. Glad as I was to see her, the sight gave me a shiver. Nothing had ever come back from underneath my bed before.

Nothing.

"Harold, you know that David has been playing this foolish game for years," said Aunt Marguerite sharply. "I don't want you to encourage it. His poor mother has enough trouble with him as it is."

"Just look under the bed," insisted Harold. "Look at the floor!"

I could have told him what would happen. In fact, now that I think of it, I *had* told him—several times—when we were younger. He just never believed me. So he was actually surprised that when he finally convinced Aunt Marguerite to get down on her knees and raise the edge of the bedspread all she saw was bare floor.

Harold and my aunt didn't stay much longer. After they left Mom yelled at me for "dragging up that stupid fantasy again."

And that was the end of things—until later that night, when Fluffy began talking to me.

She had come and curled up on my pillow when I climbed into bed, the way she often did. This had made me a little nervous, but since she had seemed perfectly normal since her reappearance, I had let her stay.

It was storming again when the big clock downstairs struck midnight. As the last chime faded, Fluffy opened her eyes.

They were red.

Now sometimes a cat's eyes will catch the light just the right way to reflect off the back of them or something, and they look red. I've seen that. I know what it looks like.

This was different. Fluffy's eyes were fire red, blazing with their own light. Before I could move, she nuzzled her face close to my ear and whispered, "Weztix wants you, David. He wants you to come to the other side."

I screamed and yanked up the covers, sending Fluffy flying off the bed.

"What's going on up there?" shouted my father.

"It's Fluffy!" I cried. "She's . . . she's . . ."

My voice trailed off as I realized that Dad would never believe me.

"She's *what?*" he yelled.

"Nothing!" I shouted. "Never mind. Forget it."

Why did I give up so easily? Because I had been through this a hundred times before. Because I had barely avoided being sent to a mental institution after I had insisted on clinging to the "delusion" that there was something strange under my bed. And most of all because I didn't know that being sent away would have been infinitely preferable to what lay in store for me.

Fluffy clawed her way back onto the bed. Her eyes blazed in the darkness.

"Go away!" I hissed. "Get out of here!"

Instead of leaving she slunk onto my chest. "Go under the bed, David," she hissed. "Wez-tix wants you under the bed."

I jumped to my feet, scooped up Fluffy, and threw her into the hall. Then I slammed the door and took a flying leap back onto my bed, avoiding at least six feet of the floor. I lay there shaking with terror, wishing I could sleep downstairs for the night. But my parents had put a stop to that one angry night years before.

After I caught my breath, I hung my head over the bed and lifted the edge of the sheet, hoping not to find anything too strange. And what I saw wasn't that strange, really. Just that familiar shimmering grayness. But it scared me now in a way it never had before.

I rolled back onto the bed and stared up into the darkness, wondering if I would make it until morning.

Suddenly I felt something pounce onto the bed. I cut short my scream when I realized it was Fluffy again.

I glanced sideways. The door was still closed.

"How did you get in here?" I whispered.

I know people talk to their pets all the time, but I realized with a kind of terrible fascination that I expected her to answer me.

"The same way I got back from the other side," she purred. "Once you've been there, doors don't mean that much. But you'd better go soon, David. They're waiting for you."

"Who?" I asked desperately. "What do they want?"

Instead of answering, Fluffy jumped to the floor and scooted under the bed. I rolled over and stuck my head down again. Heart pounding, I lifted the bedspread. My cat was gone. But the shimmering gray nothingness that had replaced my floor now had a small blue circle in the middle of it.

From the circle came a new voice. "We're waiting for you, David. Come to us. *Come to us!*"

I rolled back onto the bed, pulled the covers over my head, and tucked the sheets tightly around me, trying to convince myself I would be safe if I just stayed wrapped up that way. I have no idea why I thought that; desperation probably. Who knows? Maybe it would have worked if I hadn't fallen asleep. But when everything is dark and silent and sleep starts tugging at the edges of your mind, even terror can only keep you awake so long. Maybe I could have stayed awake if I had dared to get off the bed and move around. But lying there, wrapped in the sheets, lying still, lying silent, sleep finally claimed me.

Even then, things might have been all right if only I hadn't been such a restless sleeper. But I was a real tosser and turner, and it probably wasn't long after I fell asleep that I flopped out of my protective cocoon. It probably wasn't much longer before my arm was dangling over the edge of the bed, my fingertips brushing the floor.

I was woken by another hand, cold and damp, grabbing mine.

"Who's there?" I cried, trying to push myself up from the bed.

The cold hand linked with mine gripped me tighter, holding me in place. I screamed, loudly, not caring what my parents thought this time, not caring if I got sent away for special treatment, as long as it got me out of this room, away from this house.

I heard my parents pounding up the stairs, my father cursing as he ran. I continued to scream as loudly as I could. "Let go!" I shrieked. *"LET GO!"*

The hand began pulling harder.

"David, what's going on in there?" cried

Dad. He tried to open the door—I could hear him rattling the knob—but it wouldn't budge, despite the fact that it had no lock. "David? *DAVID!*"

"It's got me!" I screamed. "It won't let go!"

"What has you?" cried my mother. "David, what is it? What's wrong? Harvey, can't you get that door down?"

The door shuddered as my father threw himself against it, but it held solid.

Another hand grabbed my wrist, adding its strength to the first. Thrashing, twisting, fighting every inch of the way, I was drawn over the edge of the bed. I hit the floor with a thump. The hands continued to pull. Soon my arm was under the bed up to my elbows. With nothing on the floor to hold on to, nothing to give me traction, the rest of my body would soon follow.

"No!" I screamed, pushing my free hand against the side of the bed. "No! No! Let me go!"

I heard my father throw himself against the door again.

The cold hands kept pulling and pulling. I swung myself around, jamming my shoulder against the side of the bed, deciding I would rather let them pull my arm out of its socket than let them pull me under the bed.

A third time my father slammed against the door. It splintered and burst open. Too late. My bed slid across the floor to reveal the swirling gray nothingness that lay waiting beneath it. A horrible crackling filled the air as the nothingness sucked me in.

Somewhere above me, I heard my parents shouting my name.

"Now do you believe me?" I cried.

I was sinking into something like a thick, foul-smelling pudding. It was colder than anything I had ever experienced—a cold that worked its way into the deepest parts of me, penetrating to the center of my bones.

Then, suddenly, I was through the coldness and falling into dark.

The fall only lasted an instant. I landed with a dull thump against something that felt like a mattress, but turned out to be a huge fungus. Above me swirled a cool gray circle with a spot of blue in the center—the place through which I had fallen.

I could still hear my parents shouting my name.

Four torches, mounted on poles, formed a square around me. I heard an evil chuckle to my right. I turned toward it, and the flickering light provided my first sight of the creature who had dragged me here. He was foul looking, with long hair that hung around his shoulders

**14**

in greasy strings. When he beckoned to me, I saw that he had long, yellowed fingernails; when he smiled, he showed sharp, rotting teeth. His eyes glittered with malice from their deep sockets. Yet for all that, I could tell that he had once been human, which may have been the scariest thing of all.

That, and the fact that he looked oddly familiar. With a shudder, I realized I had seen him in my dreams—or, to be more accurate, in my nightmares.

"Got you at lasssst," he said in a hissing voice that was filled with deep satisfaction. "Got you at lasssst."

My terror was so deep that at first I was unable to speak. When I finally realized that he wasn't going to kill me on the spot, I asked in a trembling voice, "Who are you?"

"You mean you don't know?" he replied, sounding genuinely astonished.

I shook my head.

He laughed. "Weztix will tell you," he said, making an odd little leap. "Weztix will tell you!"

He reached for my hand. When I drew back his eyes blazed. "Stand up!" he snapped. "We're going to ssssee Weztix."

"I want to go home," I whimpered.

"Don't be ssssstupid! Now come along. I don't want to have to hurt you."

He said this last with such feeling that I actually believed him—though if I had understood just *why* he didn't want to hurt me, I might have been even more terrified than I already was.

It was a terrible journey. The place into which I had fallen was a sort of living nightmare, darkened by strange shadows that stretched and twisted around us, though I could see no source of light, nor anything to block it and cause the shadows. It was as if the darkness had a life and a mind of its own.

I could hear unpleasant noises in the distance: desperate, cackling laughter; sighs so deep they could have been made by a mountain; an odd rumbling; an occasional scream. The dank air smelled so weird I was almost afraid to breathe it.

Eyes peered out at us from the darkness. I was terrified that they might belong to some new creature that would reach out to snatch me away. (Though what could be worse than the situation I was in already is hard to imagine.) Later, unseen hands *did* pluck at me, but my captor shouted and drove them away. In several places spiderwebs stretched across our path, and since I was forced to walk in the lead, they continually wrapped themselves across my face. I shuddered each time they did. Other things, less familiar, seemed to brush over my face as well, which was even more frightening.

"Are we in hell?" I asked at one point.

The creature behind me hissed and said, "Don't be ssssilly."

We entered a cave and began to follow a series of tunnels through other caves, some small, some enormous. The tunnels were pitch-black in places, lit by torches in others. At one point we walked along a narrow path that had a rock wall on one side, an immeasurable drop on the other. Though I'm used to that path now, I was terrified at the time.

Sharp stones cut my bare feet, and they began to bleed.

Eventually I spotted a red glow ahead of us. As we drew closer, I saw that the glow came from a large cave. We walked toward it, splashing through a wide patch of muddy water where slimy things slithered over my feet. When something began nibbling on my bloody toes I cried out in fear, but my captor just pushed me forward.

We stopped at the mouth of an enormous cavern. A stone path, about three feet wide and lined with torches, led across a stretch of black water to a tall, rocky island that looked like a giant skull rising from the water.

Carved into the island's side, curving up

the jaw and around the back of the head, was a slender stairway.

On top of the skull stood Weztix.

Fluffy was sitting on his shoulder.

Weztix was far taller than a man and unbelievably beautiful, like some statue of a greek god come to life. Light seemed to pour from his face when he looked down at me.

"Welcome, David," he said in a voice that was as beautiful as he was. "Welcome. We have been waiting for you for a long time."

Though I had felt a surge of relief at seeing this beautiful creature, his words made me nervous again.

"Waiting for me?" I asked.

He chuckled. "Surely you knew *something* was waiting for you under your bed."

"I just know it scared me," I replied.

He smiled, which made his face even more beautiful. "Good. That's what this place is all about."

"What *is* this place?" I asked.

"The land of nightmares, of course," he said, spreading his arms in welcome. "And I am the Lord of Nightmares. My name is Weztix, and I am the source of all your worst dreams."

My blood felt cold in my veins. "Why . . . why have you brought me here?"

"Because we need you," he said. "And because we could."

"I don't understand."

He spread his arms, then rose into the air and began to float in my direction. I cringed as he came down, fearing that he would land on top of me and crush me. But he touched down about three feet away.

My head came up to about his kneecap.

Looking down at me, Weztix said, "There aren't many places where the border between nightmare and reality is frail enough for someone to pass through it to our side. *We* can go through, of course; we have to, in order to do our job."

As he spoke, I began to have flashbacks of old nightmares, terrifying dreams that had vanished from my conscious memory but turned out to have been lurking at the back of my mind, waiting to spring out again. Nightmares, I now understand, that had been meant to prepare me for this moment.

"The thing is," continued Weztix, "bringing new people to *this* side is a bit of a problem. Sometimes I actually run short on help. After all, the way the world is these days there are often more nightmares than I can deliver! Anyway, we've known for some time that there was a weakness under your bed—which meant that you were a candidate for a job here."

More old nightmare images came surging to the surface. I felt hot tears running down my face.

"Why?" I asked. "Is this punishment for something bad I did?"

Weztix threw back his head and laughed. "Don't give yourself airs, David! It is completely and utterly random. Not a thing you could have done to make it happen, not a thing you could have done to avoid it. It has nothing to do with you as a person. You just happened to have the wrong bedroom."

He smiled again. "I think it's scarier that way, don't you?"

I nodded solemnly.

"Anyway, weak as the boundary was beneath your bed, we still couldn't bring you through until some other living thing from your side had made the final break. When your cat came through the floor today, Timothy knew that his long wait had been rewarded."

"Timothy?"

Weztix nodded toward the evil-looking creature who had pulled me into the nightmare world. With a sick feeling, I realized that my captor was—or at least had been—a kid.

"Timothy is one of my delivery boys," said

Weztix. "Same as you will be. After all, *someone* has to pass out the nightmares."

"I don't want to!" I cried.

Weztix shook his head. "Look at it this
way, David. Most people your age don't have
any idea what they want to be when they grow
up. They muddle their way through school,
then thrash around, trying this, trying that,
wondering what to do with themselves. You
don't have to worry about any of that. Your
life's work has been chosen for you!"

He began to laugh again. This time the
sound was not so beautiful. Pushing my hands
against my ears, I threw myself to the ground
and began to sob.

It did no good. Nothing did any good. I was
a prisoner in the land of nightmares.

I don't know how much longer it was before my training began. Back then I found it
hard to measure time in this place where reality shifts so easily that not only can one day
slide into the next, but one place can slide into
another as well. Here in the land of nightmares, boundaries merge and break the way
they do in dreams. You might walk into a
small house and go through dozens or hundreds
of rooms before you find your way out. Or you
might walk through a door and find yourself in
a forest—or sit down under a tree and find

yourself having dinner with an army of the dead.

After a while you begin to learn to look past those things. You can move fast down here once you know the shortcuts. And you do have to move fast to do your job.

I hate my job. It works like this: Weztix calls me and I go to sit with him inside the stone skull, in a dark chamber that smells of loss and suffering, and sometimes of death. He closes one huge hand over my head and fills my brain with images.

Sometimes when he takes his hand away I realize that I've been screaming. So I won't talk about those images right now. But maybe you've seen them anyway; maybe you've *dreamed* them. Because what I do when Weztix is finished with me is carry the things he's poured in my head back to the real world.

Which is to say, I climb the ladders of nightmare and come up underneath your bed. Now that I'm one of Weztix's messengers, I can cross the barrier easily. And once I've risen up beneath your bed, I lie there in the darkness beneath you and whisper to you while you sleep, spinning back the images that Weztix has planted in my brain.

Why don't I try to run away one of those nights?

If I told you, you might never sleep again.

And I need you to sleep.

After all, if you don't sleep, how can I do my job?

The only good thing about all this was the nightmares I got to take to Harold. Heh. The truth is, I took him a lot that weren't meant for him, which is sort of against the rules. But I don't do it anymore. I pretty much stopped after they took him away for special treatment.

I used to be a good boy. I want to be good again, but I don't know if that's possible anymore. Because the only way out is for me to do what Timothy did, what all the others do eventually, and find someone to take my place.

Of course, Timothy didn't get to leave right away. As Weztix said, there's a labor shortage down here. But his reward for recruiting me was to be allowed to go back to the land of the living about ten years after I got here.

That's what I'd like to do someday. After all, I've been down here delivering nightmares for nearly thirty years now. The thing is, being a messenger of darkness and fear is the kind of work that twists a guy.

I'm not the person I used to be.

Even so, I dream of going back to the other side to stay.

It won't be long now. I've found a weakness in the boundary between the worlds. It's not as good as the one under my bed was, at least not yet. But it will be when I'm done with it. A place where someone real, someone living, could pass through into this world.

It's under a bed, of course.

Maybe yours.

The thing is, I'll feel funny about pulling another kid down here to take my place. After all, he or she won't be any happier doing this than I am.

That's why I sent this dream to the person who's writing this story. I figure if I send a warning, if I give kids a fighting chance to save themselves, I won't have to feel so bad when I finally do bring one of them down here.

Well, there it is. Now you know what might be waiting under your bed. You know what can happen if you don't get out.

Whether you do anything about it or not—well, that's up to you. But I've done my time. Sooner or later someone—maybe you—is going to take my place.

Sweet dreams. . . .

*Did you ever think about how strange mirrors really are? Strange, and somewhat . . . scary?*

# THROUGH THE MIRROR

## Anne Mazer

What would you do if your world disappeared? If it hung shining like a bit of water suspended from a leaf, and then the wind blew and shattered it on the ground? The walls of your room suddenly dissolved and you were standing in a forest, a dark forest with waving ferns? What would you do then?

Actually, it happened like this. Sandra was sitting in her bedroom staring into the mirror. She was a pretty girl, with flushed cheeks and curly fine hair with a green ribbon pinned on the side. But her face had an expression of shock, disbelief. Because the face that stared back out of the mirror was different from hers. The hair was thick and tangled. The face was dirty.

"And I just washed," Sandra muttered to herself. She wondered if the mirror was dirty.

She rubbed it a bit, and the girl on the other side put up an arm as if to protect herself.

Sandra stopped and stared. The dirty girl dropped her arm and grinned. Sandra recoiled a little, but then leaned forward. "Who are you?" she asked. "What are you doing here?"

"What are you doing here?" the dirty girl mimicked.

Sandra held up her hand as if to push the other deeper into the mirror.

The dirty girl pushed back.

"Go away!" Sandra said. "Leave me alone!"

The other reached forward, and yanked her into the mirror.

Sandra saw a flash of pink that could have been her bedspread. She saw the girl with the tangled hair leap through a silvery door that seemed to melt into the air. And then her room was gone. She was in a forest. A dark forest with curling ferns tipped with light.

She found herself on a path: a twisted, gnarled path full of pine needles and pine-cones, thorny branches, shriveled apples, and tiny blackened stones. The sky was very high above, bits of blue falling through the over-hanging trees like scraps of ragged cloth. Sandra sat down in the midst of the path, put her face in her hands, and cried.

Meanwhile, in a small yellow house, a girl with tangled hair was washing her dirty face.

She picked up a brush and brushed her hair. She fastened a ribbon—a red ribbon—in her curls.

When she looked in the mirror, she smiled. The mirror image smiled back. The red ribbon bobbed in her curly fine hair. Her cheeks were flushed and her eyes sparkled. She leaned over, tied her sneakers, and skipped down the stairs.

*People who break into other people's houses*
*may find more than they expected.*

# THE BOY WHO CRIED DRAGON

## Deborah Millitello

The doorknob turned easily. Jimmy couldn't believe his luck. Only the fifth house he'd tried in the neighborhood. No car in the garage. Excitement pulsed through him, just like before. He had broken into three other places in the past month. Not to steal anything; he didn't need to steal, not with ready access to Mom and Dad's credit cards. No, he did it the first time to prove to his friends he could, to prove he was invincible. Now he didn't want to stop. He needed the thrill of that brush with danger.

There was a small pet flap at the bottom of the door. Jimmy frowned a moment. If it was for a cat, there was no problem; the cat would be out at night. If it was for a dog, though, he didn't want to tangle with the animal, no matter how small it was. Jimmy pushed the back door open just a bit, shined his flashlight through the crack, and peeked in. Just to the right of the door was a litter box. Definitely a cat. Jimmy relaxed and slipped his short, thin body inside.

It was quiet, no sound but the squeak of his Airwalks on the vinyl floor. A dim yellow light glowed above the wooden kitchen table. The room was neat, no dishes in the sink. A bowl of cat food sat on the floor and a bag of Meow Mix on the counter. The white double-door fridge was filled with an assortment of food and drink; leftovers here, a few fruits and vegetables there, mostly meat in the freezer. He helped himself to a canned cola, smiled as he popped the tab, and walked down the short hallway, past the stairs on the left.

The lights popped on when he entered the living room. Throat dry, skin cold, he jumped back, spilling soda on his black hooded jacket. Immediately, the lights went out. He edged back into the room, and the lights came on again. "Must be some new gadget," he mumbled as his heart slowed to near normal.

Little hearts, diamonds, spades, and clubs were woven into the thick, closed curtains and the upholstery. The carpet was bottom-of-a-well black. Torch-shaped lights hung on either side of a black-and-white marble fireplace. A large TV sat in one corner, but there was no VCR, no stereo system, not even a Walkman lying around. Not that he really wanted a Walkman; he had three at home. He just wanted something to prove to the guys he'd been here.

The other side of the room opened to a library, heavy wood shelves filled with old books. The desk was cluttered with papers, pens, and a collection of pewter and plaster figures—dragons, unicorns, fairies, and some creatures Jimmy had never seen before. The place smelled of age and old leather. He shrugged and headed back to the hall for the stairs.

The dark wood banister was smooth and warm and spoke of years of polishing with lemon-scented wax. It reminded him of Grandma: Her place always smelled like that. The same black carpet as in the living room flowed up the stairs. The stairs creaked as he climbed.

Jimmy reached the top and looked down a hallway that ended in a closed door. Four other doors, all shut, led off the hall.

He opened the first door on the left. Lights snapped on automatically, just as in the living room, and revealed a rose-pink bathroom, spotless and clean, with a bare medicine cabinet, neatly folded towels, and barely used soap. Across the hall from the bathroom, a narrow door opened to a linen closet filled with new towels and sheets. The next door led to a bedroom with rows of tiny bottles on a shelf, nothing worth stealing. Opposite was an empty room without even dust on the wooden floor. The air was stale and had a faint tinge of something. Smoke, spice, maybe perfume—Jimmy couldn't quite put his finger on exactly what, but the scent seemed out of place in there.

The last door, the one at the end of the hall, revealed a pale green room with a dark wooden four-poster bed, a chest of drawers, a dresser, and an oval gilt-framed mirror. A foot-long wooden box shaped like a treasure chest sat on the dresser.

Jimmy smiled as he hurried over to the box. It was held shut by a tiny gold padlock. Jimmy pulled on the lock, but it stayed in place. "Heck with it," he muttered, set down his soda, took out his pocket knife, and tried to pry off the little lock. He twisted, turned, pounded; finally, the lock cracked, broke, and fell off with a sound as loud as thunder.

Jimmy jumped, then crouched with his knife poised to defend himself. His eyes darted around the room, but nothing else happened. He blew out his breath, turned back to the chest, pushed up the lid, and gasped.

Inside were silver and gold rings, bracelets, necklaces, and chains, all glittering with jewels and gems. He ran his fingers through the jewelry. Was it all real? He stared for a moment, then stuffed it all into the pockets of his jacket and went back to the hall.

He had started downstairs with his prize when he heard a sound: low, barely audible, like the whoosh of a revolving door. For a split second he feared the owner had come home. He listened for a long moment, but heard nothing except a throbbing in his ears and realized he was holding his breath.

Cold sweat trickled down his forehead. His stomach twitched nervously. Bracing one hand on the wall, the other on the banister, Jimmy tiptoed down the stairs. The living room was dark, no sounds or shadows. *I'm outta here,* he thought, and sprinted for the dimly lit kitchen.

A low growl startled Jimmy. He flattened himself against the refrigerator doors and zigzagged the flashlight around the kitchen, his eyes frantically searching the shadows. He saw no one, no movement. He started inching toward the back door. The growl grew louder, closer. Jimmy grabbed a long-handled skillet from a pot rack on the wall and held it like a baseball bat.

"I'm not afraid of you," Jimmy said, although his hands shook as much as his voice.

Eyes blinked in the dark near the floor, yellow eyes with each pupil shaped like a magnifying lens viewed sideways. Jimmy turned the flashlight on the eyes. There by the door stood a house cat, black and gold, sleek and shiny.

A cat. Jimmy laughed at himself. Scared by a cat. If the guys ever found out . . .

He started to walk toward the back door again, but kept the skillet ready in case the cat tried to claw him.

"What are you doing in my house?" a bass voice boomed.

Jimmy wheeled around, looking for the speaker. No one was there.

"I said, what are you doing in my house?"

Jimmy's hand tightened on the skillet. "Where are you?"

"Here, thief."

"Where?" Jimmy cried.

The cat took a step forward and smiled.

Smiled? Jimmy shook his head. *No way,* he thought. *You're losing it, Jimmy.*

He swung the skillet at the cat, which nimbly sidestepped the blow. Jimmy grabbed the doorknob. He turned it, pulled, but nothing happened. He jerked it, yanked as hard as he could, kicked it, pounded and yelled at it. The door didn't budge.

Jimmy turned and ran for the living room, but the cat blocked his way. It was bigger now, the size of a half-grown collie, and its fur was slicked down against its body. Jimmy swung the skillet at it again. The cat batted it out of Jimmy's grasp with talons that left deep furrows in the metal.

Jimmy gasped. The cat's feet were no longer soft, padded paws. On each foot, three scaly toes stretched forward and one back. Golden-edged scales crept up the legs, covered the tail, armored the growing back, sides, and belly. The long neck had two parallel lines of horny ridges from the top of the wide head to the tip of the serpentine tail. And the head—a huge scaly triangle of smoking nostrils and daggerlike teeth.

Jimmy stared, mouth desert dry and hanging open. The creature was gigantic, way too big to fit inside the kitchen, much less the house. That's when he noticed that the painted walls were shimmering, sliding away to walls of dark stone, rough and uncut, like the walls of a cave. The ceiling was as high as that of a cathedral, with a hole at the top where moonlight dripped through. A cold breeze brushed his face. The taste of ashes filled his mouth.

"Now, thief," the bass voice echoed through the cavern, "return my treasure."

Jimmy gazed up at a black-and-gold dragon, bigger than a Learjet. Smoke twirled lazily from two broad nostrils, and a black forked tongue flicked out at Jimmy. No, it wasn't a dragon, it couldn't be! Dragons were fairy tales!

"The soda—there must've been something in the soda," Jimmy muttered.

"I did not mind that you took a soda," the dragon said, "which was not tampered with, by the way. I *was* annoyed that you came to my house uninvited, especially when I was not here to greet you. But when you broke into my chest, that angered me. Return my treasure, boy, or I will eat you." The dragon grinned miles of teeth. "I may eat you anyway."

"You're not real!" Jimmy said. "This place isn't real!"

The dragon crept closer. "Of course, it is real. Where else would a dragon live but in a cave?"

"But I was in a house." Jimmy backed up a couple of steps. "I *know* I was!"

The dragon snickered, strands of smoke rising from its nose and intertwining. "Yes, it looked very real, did it not? The human wizard I keep to mind the house for me does an excellent job."

"But you're not real!"

The dragon smiled a very unpleasant smile. "Most people think that. I try to keep it that way." The smile faded. "Now, boy, give me back my treasure."

Jimmy couldn't believe this was happening to him. "You can't be real, you can't be real!" he cried. He spun around and dove into a tun-

nel directly behind him. His flashlight barely illuminated the slick rock floor just in front of his feet. The jewelry in his jacket flopped hard against his thigh as he ran. The narrow passage bent left, dipped down, then back up, bent left again, then turned sharply left, opening into a large cavern.

Jimmy screeched to a halt. There was the dragon again, right in front of him. Cold sweat trickled down Jimmy's neck, and he retreated until he felt rough stone pressing against his back.

"You did not think that you would get away from me, did you, boy?" the dragon purred.

Jimmy looked side to side, then sprinted for another opening just a few feet to his right. The dragon laughed. Jimmy ran and ran, stumbled, and ran some more, past glowing green moss, over slime-slick rock. Something metal clinked on the rock floor. A ring or bracelet fallen from his pocket? Jimmy didn't stop to find out. He just kept running.

The path rose gradually, then leveled off. Suddenly Jimmy slipped on the slimy rocks and tumbled down a steep incline, through a doorway to a large cavern—the same cavern he'd fled!

The dragon was waiting for him, eyes narrowed. A single flap of its wings slammed

Jimmy to the floor. "There is no escape, boy. Now give me my treasure!"

Jimmy rose slowly. He put his shaking hands into his pockets, pulled out the jewelry, and tossed all of it as close to the dragon as he could throw. "There! Okay? So let me outta here. Please?"

The treasure glittered as the dragon gathered it in one claw, sniffed it, breathed in deep, then carefully placed it on top of a huge heap of other gold and gems. The dragon turned back to Jimmy and stretched its giant head down until their faces were only inches apart. Jimmy's eyes watered and burned from the dragon's breath.

"For the rest of your life," the dragon rumbled in his face, "I will haunt your days. I will stalk your dreams. I will be in every shadow. My eyes will see you in the darkest night. If you ever break into another house, I will know it and I will come for you. Do you understand?"

Eyes popping, Jimmy gulped, shivered down to his toes, and nodded.

"And now, boy"—the dragon gave him a toothy grin—"I am hungry . . . and you smell like dinner."

A shriek bubbled out of Jimmy's mouth. He wheeled and ran to another tunnel, higher and wider than the others, slick with moss and

water. The passage twisted right, left, and right
again. He tripped and fell down a sharp slide,
scratching his face. The flashlight slipped from
his hand, rolled away, and blinked out. He was
alone in the dark—alone, winded, and terrified.

"Do you enjoy excitement, danger?" came
the dragon's voice close, too close, behind him.
"Is this dangerous enough for you, boy? Is this
enough excitement?"

Fear surged through Jimmy like fire, spur-
ring his legs into motion. He jumped to his feet
and headed away from the dragon. The path rose
steeply; he slipped halfway up and scraped his
hands raw. He ran as fast as he could in the
dark, left hand touching the wall of the tunnel,
right hand weaving in front of him. Running,
running, stumbling over fallen stones and stepping into sudden pools. His clothes were torn,
muddy, and soaked with icy water. His chest
hurt as he sucked in air and his muscles
cramped from the damp cold.

The roar of the dragon drove Jimmy faster,
faster, on and up until he saw a pinpoint of
light ahead. He ran until he thought his muscles would tear apart, his lungs burst, his
heart explode. But he didn't stop, not with the
light so close ahead and the dragon so close
behind.

He scrambled up a scree-covered slope.
Rocks slid from under his feet, pebbles shifted,

pitched him to his knees, sliced into his palms. *Move, keep going, stay ahead of the dragon.* The smell of smoke was so thick, Jimmy thought he'd choke to death. *One more step, just one more step.* There! Just in front of him! The light, the light! He'd made it! The light— the red and white flashing lights.

Hands grabbed Jimmy and forced him face-down on the ground. "Don't let him get me!" he wheezed into the damp grass. "Keep him away!"

"Spread 'em," said a gruff voice. "Hands on your head."

Another pair of hands ran down his sides, down the inseams and the outside of his legs, in his jacket pockets. "Nothing."

"You live here?" the gruff policeman asked.

Jimmy tried to answer, but he was still out of breath and exhausted. It hurt just to suck in air.

Just then a car drove up, and a white-haired man in a business suit stepped out. "What's happening?" he asked as he hurried across the lawn. "This is my house." He pulled out his wallet and showed his driver's license to the officers.

"Break-in, suspected burglary," the gruff cop said. "A neighbor reported strange sounds and lights going on and off in your house. We caught this punk running out the front door."

"You'd think a neighborhood like this would be safe from thugs." The old man shook his head and glared at Jimmy. "No place is safe anymore."

"Cuff him," said the gruff policeman. "You have the right to remain silent. Anything you say . . ."

The other cop pulled Jimmy's wrists together behind his back and slipped the hard plastic loops around them. Both cops pulled Jimmy to his feet.

At that moment, a black-and-gold cat jumped from the shadows and clawed Jimmy's leg. Jimmy howled. The cat leaped away and sprang into the old man's arms.

"There now, Dragon," the old man cooed as he stroked the cat's fur, "did that bad little burglar scare you?"

"Dragon?" Jimmy cried. "Its name is Dragon?"

"Yes," the old man said sharply.

"But . . . it *is* a dragon."

The gruff policeman leaned in close to Jimmy's face. "Are you giving up the right to remain silent?"

"No!" Jimmy said, and nodded toward the cat. "But it changed into a dragon! I saw it! It chased me all through the house, and the house turned into caves and tunnels, it kept chasing and chasing me, and it was going to eat me! Don't let it get me, please! It's not a cat! It's a real freaking dragon!"

"Great," muttered the other cop, "another insanity plea."

"But it *is* a dragon!" Jimmy shouted. "Was a dragon! I'm not crazy! I'm not!"

"Come on," said the gruff cop. The two officers pulled Jimmy to the squad car, bent his head down, eased him in, and closed the door behind him. The cops got in the front seat, the gruff one driving, the other reporting in on the radio.

Jimmy stared out the window at the old man and his cat. Yellow eyes blinked at Jimmy. A wisp of smoke curled from the cat's nose, and a black forked tongue flicked out. The old man held out his hand and took a lit pipe from thin air. He puffed it once. Then old man and cat both smiled smugly at Jimmy.

"Look!" Jimmy screamed. "See? I told you! It's a dragon! A dragon!"

The gruff cop chuckled as he drove away. "Tell it to the judge, kid."

Jimmy huddled in the backseat, miserable, scared, and hopeless. Fat chance a judge would believe him. No one would, not his mom and dad, not his friends, no one. Why did he have to pick that house? He'd never do it again, never, never, never.

Suddenly, Jimmy heard a voice inside his head, the bass voice of the dragon. "Remember me, boy, and remember well what I told you." There was a pause, a sound of smacking lips and of glittering jewels being sifted and falling, then, "I know your smell. And I never forget a smell."

*This is a strange and disturbing story, not scary in the ways that we usually think of scary, yet probably the most truly nightmarish tale of any in this book.*

# DRAWING THE MOON

## Janni Lee Simner

Andrew knew that the moon had stolen his parents away.

He had tried to explain to Elizabeth once, after the funeral, but she didn't understand. Her face had turned horribly pale, and she whispered, "They're dead, Andrew. Don't you know that?" And then, just in case he didn't, she drew him a picture. She used all her red pencils and some of Andrew's crayons, besides. She used rusty-red for the brick buildings, brownish-red for the mugger's jacket, rosy-red for Mom's torn sweater on the sidewalk. And bright red for Dad, where the knife had gone through his chest.

Andrew tore up the drawing, not because

looking at it sent icy shivers up his spine, though it did, but because she'd gotten the drawing all wrong. She'd left out the moon, large and round in the night sky, and that was the most important part.

Even though she was older than him, Elizabeth didn't remember. But Andrew did. He remembered how silver moonlight had reflected off the knife. He remembered how the moonlight had bubbled up from the cracks in the sidewalk, pulling Dad to the ground. He remembered how streams of moonlight had flowed over Mom, already facedown on the pavement, keeping her from getting up. And he remembered how the light had turned brighter and brighter, until his eyes hurt so much he had to close them. That was when he'd screamed. It was also when the police had come running, their footsteps hard and loud against the street.

When Andrew had opened his eyes again, the light was gone. A policeman stood on the sidewalk, twisting the mugger's arms behind his back. Another policeman knelt in front of Elizabeth, talking in a low, sad voice. A siren wailed down the street. Somewhere, very far away, a girl laughed in the darkness.

Andrew had known, then, that his parents were gone. Not dead, though the policeman had used that word over and over. Stolen. That was a different thing entirely.

# Drawing the Moon

*   *   *

After the funeral, Andrew and Elizabeth moved to the country to live with their grandfather. The woods were quiet; Andrew liked that. A hurt had started deep in his chest the night his parents were taken. The woods were the only place that could make the hurt go away, at least for a little while. Although she didn't say so, Andrew knew Elizabeth felt the same way. She spent a lot of time outside, drawing the trees and the river.

At night, though, they had to come back inside, and that was harder. Dinner was bad enough, and the time they spent sitting in front of the television afterward, with nothing to do but watch the flickering pictures, was worse. But bedtime was the hardest time of all.

Andrew's room had a row of high windows. On clear nights the moon shone through them so brightly that Andrew could see the dark trunks of the trees stretching toward the sky. As long as the moon stayed outside, though, it didn't bother him. He could still close his eyes and go to sleep.

But when he left his windows open—something his grandfather insisted on, at least for hot summer nights—the wind blew through the screen, brushing his cheek and tugging at the blankets. Sometimes, the wind whispered his name. And it did something else, too. It took the moonlight from outside and blew it into his room.

The moonlight was cold, and it got down into Andrew's bones; no matter how hot the night was or how many blankets he wrapped himself in, he couldn't stop shivering. But the cold wasn't half as bad as the pictures.

Once the light got in, it snaked up the walls, hundreds of little silver strands of it, and the strands wove themselves into pictures.

The pictures were of his parents. They showed Andrew the night Mom and Dad had disappeared, over and over, until the hurt in his chest got so bad he thought he would explode. He tried closing his eyes, but even through closed eyelids he could see the scenes the moon painted—all in silver, with none of Elizabeth's colors, but sharp and real just the same. He saw Mom and Dad walking down the city street, holding hands, Elizabeth and Andrew just behind them. He saw the mugger jump out of the shadows. He saw Mom being hit and falling to the ground, where her head smashed against the pavement. He saw the knife go through Dad's chest.

But in the pictures, Mom died of the falling, and Dad died of the stabbing. That wasn't right at all.

The moon had stolen Andrew's parents. So why would it draw him pictures in which that hadn't happened, in which other things had happened instead? Andrew wondered about that for many nights before he came up with an answer.

The moon didn't want him to know what it had done. Or now that he knew, it wanted him to forget.

Andrew couldn't make the pictures go away, and he wouldn't stop believing what he knew was true. So as the summer wore on, he slept less and less at night, and felt more and more tired and grumpy during the day. The hurt in his chest was still there, too. He didn't think it would ever go away.

He had to do something. After thinking a long time, he decided he had to catch the moon. He'd lock it away, and then it wouldn't bother him ever again.

He didn't tell Elizabeth. He knew, somehow, that she would think the idea was silly, that she would insist the moon couldn't be caught. But if the moon could get into his room in the first place, then somehow, Andrew knew, he could trap it. He just had to figure out how.

He thought of the silver light reflecting off the silver blade as Dad fell. Maybe the moon liked silver. As soon as he thought that, he knew it was right, though he couldn't say why.

He searched the house for something silver, something with space inside and a latch to keep it closed. The only thing he found was a tarnished silver box, with flowers carved around the edges, under his grandfather's bed. The box was filled with things that used to belong to Andrew's grandmother: a gold watch, a faded blue ribbon, a tiny locket. Andrew felt a little guilty as he pulled them out. He put everything but the box back under the bed as neatly as he could.

He took the box into his room, hiding it under his pillow. And then he waited for dinner to be over and for night to come.

The wind started as soon as he turned out the lights. "Andrew," it whispered. "Andrew."

Andrew buried his head under the covers, pretending to be asleep. He clutched the box close to his chest.

He knew when the moon had come in, because all of a sudden he was cold, shivering so hard that his teeth chattered. He didn't want to get out from under the covers, not ever.

He took a deep breath, then poked his head out. The entire room was filled with light, so bright that if someone turned on the lamp, he wasn't sure he'd notice. On the walls, the light had already started forming pictures. He could just make out Mom's long hair, Dad's bearded face. He almost reached out to them, but he pulled his hand away. They were only pictures, not real. Touching them wouldn't change that. Andrew swallowed. His throat felt suddenly dry.

He reached under the covers and pulled out the box. He opened the lid, held the box out toward one of the walls—the one beneath the windows—and waited.

At first, nothing happened. For a moment Andrew thought he heard laughter, but a moment later he decided he'd imagined it.

He cast the covers aside. The cold raised goose bumps on his arms and turned his fingers as numb as if he were holding a snowball. He stood, clutching the box between his hands. He walked to the wall and touched the box against it.

The picture of his parents flickered, like a movie going out of focus. Andrew just stood there, shivering. His toes were cold now, too, so cold he couldn't feel them.

Another flicker, and then a lick of moonlight leapt toward the box like a silver flame. Suddenly moonlight was streaming down the walls, hundreds of thin, liquid rivers of it, all of them flowing into the box. The box pulsed between Andrew's hands, icy cold. He fought not to drop it, even though his fingers froze against the metal.

Then, just as suddenly as it had started, it

stopped. The room was dark, darker than it had ever been. It was warm, too; Andrew's fingers and toes tingled as if he'd just come in out of the snow.

He quickly shut and latched the box.

Outside, rain pattered against the roof. There was no moonlight, no moon. Elizabeth might have blamed that on the rain. Andrew knew better.

For the box in his hands pulsed with light, far too bright for tarnished silver.

Andrew smiled. He slid the box under his bed. Then he crawled back under the covers and slept soundly for the first time in a long, long while.

The light didn't bother him after that; the sky remained moonless and dark. Something else troubled him, though.

Beneath his bed, within the silver box, the moon started weeping. The sound began so softly he thought he was imagining it, but it got louder every night. It was the last sound Andrew heard when he fell asleep, and the first when he woke up. It followed him into his dreams.

At first he thought it was an awful trick, the moon trying to make him feel sorry for it after all it had done. But after a while, curiosity got the best of him, and he pulled the box out from under the bed. He meant only to glance at it, to make sure the lid was still safely closed.

The light had disappeared. This startled him so much that he set the box down on the bed to get a closer look. The silver was ordinary tarnished silver, nothing more. Yet Andrew could still hear the crying, not soft at all now, the sort of choking sobs that make it hard to breathe. Andrew couldn't help himself. He unlatched the lid and cracked it open just a tiny bit.

A wind started up, first a low whistle, then a sudden, icy gust. The box flew from Andrew's hands onto the floor. The lid clattered open. He saw a flash of light, gone before he could even cover his eyes. Then the wind died as quickly as it had begun. Andrew looked across the room, trying to figure out what had happened.

A girl stood by the windows, looking back at him.

She wore old jeans, faded and torn at the knees, and a short-sleeved green sweater. Her hair fell in two dark braids down her back. Her eyes were red and swollen, as if she really had been crying.

"You're just a kid," Andrew said.

The girl brushed a hand across her face. Her voice, when she spoke, sounded cross, not sad like he thought it would. "What did you expect? The moon herself?"

"Yes," Andrew said.

The girl laughed, then, a bitter sound. Ice trickled down Andrew's spine. The night his parents were taken, he'd heard that same laugh.

"Did you think the moon could be held in a box as small as that? All you caught was the moon's poor messenger." The girl's voice dropped to a whisper. "And I'm sure I'll be punished for being gone so long." She pulled her thin arms around herself.

For a moment Andrew stared at her, not sure what to say. Then he asked very softly, "Am I right? Does the moon really have Mom and Dad?"

"Of course she does." The girl sounded annoyed again. "And if you have any sense at all, you'll forget about it as soon as you can. Sooner, even. Humans aren't supposed to know about these things, that's what the moon always says. You won't have any peace until you forget. Nor will I, for that matter. Do you know how much work it is, carrying all that light back and forth, making all those pictures?"

Andrew didn't care how much work it was. What he did care about was that he'd been right. Mom and Dad had really been stolen.

He'd known that, of course, but being told for sure still made him feel strange.

"Can you bring me to them?"

The girl laughed again. "You're a fool," she said. "I don't think I knew what a fool really was until I met you."

"But can you?" To see Mom and Dad, for real and not in a picture, even for a very short time—Andrew was sure the hurt in his chest would go away, if only he could do that.

"Of course I can do it. But I've sense enough that I won't."

"Why not?" Andrew couldn't bear to come so close and then not see them.

"Go to sleep," the girl said. "Forget you ever saw me, forget there's such a thing as moonlight that can make pictures on your walls. Go to sleep and live your safe, normal human life. The moon will leave you alone, if only you do that."

"No." Andrew took a step toward her. "If you don't take me to them, I'll put you back in the box next time you come. And I won't ever let you out again."

"Oh, I'd get out. I did this time, after all."

"But it would take a long time." Andrew hesitated, trying to remember something she'd said. "And you'd be punished. Probably worse than you're going to be punished now."

The girl rubbed her hands along her arms.

"Yes," she whispered. And then she said, "I can take you, if you want. But you shouldn't want it. You don't know what can happen."

"I don't care."

More laughter. "Oh, you will. But I've given you fair warning. That's all I have to do. Now any mistakes you make are your own."

She reached out and took Andrew's hand. Her grip was cold and smooth; Andrew had to twine his fingers around hers to make sure his hand didn't slip away.

The girl took a deep breath and closed her eyes. Her feet left the ground so slowly that Andrew didn't notice at first. It took him even longer to notice that he was floating upward, too. He realized he was still in his pajamas, and barefoot as well. He wondered if he should have changed his clothes. It was too late now, though. They were almost at the window.

"You have to pull away the screen," Andrew said.

"No I don't." The girl passed through the window screen as easily as she'd floated through the room. Andrew expected to fall to the floor as soon as the screen touched him, but he didn't. He didn't feel the screen at all. He slid through, into the dark night. Raindrops glistened on the leaves of the trees. The rain was still falling, but he couldn't feel that, either.

They floated, farther and farther from

home, until the lights of his grandfather's house turned to flickering specks and disappeared. All that Andrew saw were dark clouds moving across a darker sky. There was no moon, not that he could see.

Silence surrounded them, so heavy Andrew's ears hurt. To break the silence, he asked the girl, "Do you have a name?"

For a long time she didn't answer, and Andrew thought maybe she hadn't heard. But then she looked at him and said, "Yes, I do. Not that there's anyone to use it anymore." Her voice sounded strangely sad. "My name is Lydia."

"But that's a normal name," Andrew said, not sure what sort of name he'd expected her to have.

"Of course it is." Lydia's voice turned sharp. "I was a normal kid once, too."

She turned away from him and wouldn't say anything more.

Andrew lost track of how long they floated. It could have been five minutes. It could have been forever. After a time, though, the wind picked up. It tugged at the edges of Andrew's pajamas and pulled at his arms. He tightened his grip on Lydia's hand until his knuckles hurt. The wind whipped about his legs and it shoved his feet out from under him. Andrew tried to pull himself back up, but instead he started falling, faster and faster, head and feet tumbling over each other. Lydia's hand slid out from his own. He tried to scream, but he couldn't hear his own voice.

The clouds parted. Suddenly silver light was everywhere, so bright that Andrew couldn't tell up from down. He just kept falling, and even when he closed his eyes, the light was still with him. The cold was there, too. It cut through Andrew's pajamas, straight down to his bones. If he'd rolled naked in the snow, he couldn't have felt any colder.

Then he hit the ground so hard his teeth rattled. For a while he just lay there, staring into the light, not sure whether his eyes were open or closed. He reached out and touched his face. He couldn't see his hand, even when he pushed it right against his eyeballs.

"Get up," Lydia whispered. He couldn't see her, either. "That's no way to present yourself, not here." She took his hand and helped him to his feet. He looked around, but all he saw was silver light.

A voice cut through the brightness. "Lydia." The voice was still, softer than anything Andrew had ever heard, but he couldn't have ignored it if he'd tried. "You're late, Lydia." The words wrapped themselves around Andrew, slid into the space between his ears, brushed against his cheek like silk. He couldn't move, not while that voice spoke.

"I know," Lydia said. Her voice shook.

"There is a price you must pay for being late."

"I know." She gave Andrew's hand a tight, frightened squeeze. He felt sorry suddenly for her.

"Will you go on your own?" the voice asked.

A moment's hesitation. And then, very quickly, "Yes. I'll go." Lydia dropped Andrew's hand.

He didn't hear her walk away, but it didn't matter. He couldn't see her, and he couldn't feel her holding his hand. He was alone. A cold wind blew. He shivered.

"Andrew." The voice caressed him, held him in place. "Why are you here, Andrew?"

Andrew swallowed. "Because I want to see Mom and Dad," he whispered.

"What makes you think I can show them to you?"

"Because you're the moon," Andrew said. And then, suddenly unsure, he asked, "You are the moon, aren't you?"

"That's one word you can use. There are others."

"Like what?"

"Like sleep. Or death."

"But Mom and Dad aren't dead! They're just stolen!" Andrew yelled as loud as he could, but his voice stayed a squeaky whisper.

The voice laughed, a cold, velvety sound that sent goose bumps up Andrew's arms. "Maybe dead and stolen are the same thing."

"No!" Andrew shouted. "No! There's a difference!" Dead things, he knew, were gone forever. But stolen things—sometimes you could get stolen things back again.

"I want Mom and Dad back."

"They're mine," the moon said.

"No. Take someone else. But give them back."

More laughter. If Andrew could have moved at all, he would have run away.

"Who would you suggest I take?"

Andrew thought about that. "The man with the knife. Take him."

"That would be fair," the velvet voice said. "But that's only one person. I need two."

"Now you've done it," Lydia hissed. She was still beside him after all—or maybe she'd left and come back. "The moon wants *you* now. Can't you tell?"

"Do you?" Andrew asked. He wished there were somewhere in the brightness he could hide.

"That would be fair."

"No," Andrew said. He couldn't imagine

staying here, not forever, and he knew that was what the moon was asking. He started shivering, and once he started he couldn't stop. He pulled his arms around himself. He realized that he could move again, but he also realized that it didn't matter. The light was all around him; everything looked the same. Where could he go?

He shivered in the silence for a long time. Finally he spoke, as much to hear his own voice as anything else.

"If I stayed, would you let Mom and Dad go?"

The voice cut through the silence, smooth as butter. "I said I would."

"That's not what I asked."

A chuckle. "I promise," the moon said, her voice mocking and low. "I will return them. Do you wish to see them before they leave?"

"I didn't say I'd do it." Andrew needed time to think, to decide.

"Didn't you?" No laughter this time. Andrew realized with a shudder that the moon was right. He'd decided, inside at least. If he went back, things would be different. His parents wouldn't be stolen anymore; they'd be dead. He couldn't let that happen. Even if it meant the moon would take him instead.

"All right. I'll do it." As Andrew spoke, he felt the hurt in his chest dissolve, suddenly and completely. It was replaced by something worse. Something hard and cold and terribly lonely. Andrew wanted to run to his bedroom and hide beneath the covers, though a small corner of his mind told him he couldn't do that, not anymore.

"Do you wish to speak to them before they go?"

Andrew thought about that, but in the end decided against it. He wasn't sure he could bear watching them leave a second time.

"All right, then," the moon said, and she didn't say anything more. She left Andrew alone, trembling in the cold silver light.

In the distance, Andrew realized, he could make out faint figures: Lydia, and with her, two taller people—Mom and Dad. All at once he changed his mind and ran toward them. He ran as fast as he could, but the harder he ran, the farther away his parents became—until they were gone, gone once and for all. He tried to cry, but the tears froze on his face and disappeared.

The wind began to blow again, with a low, moaning sound that cut through to Andrew's bones. It tugged at his hair, and when he tried to twist away, it pulled harder, not letting go until he screamed. Then it stopped abruptly. Andrew fell to his knees, onto the smooth, hard ground he couldn't see.

"Andrew," the moon whispered. "You're mine now, Andrew. You'll do whatever I say, whenever I say. There are prices you'll pay, if you ever do anything wrong."

Andrew buried his face in his hands. Light pulsed against his eyelids. He had no tears, but he cried anyway, dry, painful sobs that clawed at him inside. Laughter started up, soft as velvet, from all directions at once. Against his will, Andrew rocked with the rhythmic sound.

The moon kept laughing. And this time, Andrew knew, it laughed at him.

There's a window in Elizabeth's room, and on clear nights the moon shines in, round and bright. The light is so strong she can see the city buildings stretching toward the sky. If she leaves her window open, the wind blows through the screen, tugging at her blankets and whispering her name. And it does something else, too. It takes the moonlight from outside and blows it into her room.

The light is cold, and it gets down into Elizabeth's bones. But the cold isn't half as bad as the pictures, drawn in silver moonlight on the walls.

Because she can't sleep on nights like this, Elizabeth gets up and draws some pictures of her own. She uses lots of red pencils—red for the mugger's jacket, red for the brick apartments, red for Andrew, where the knife went through his chest. But she uses silver pencils, too. And she never leaves out the moon, because that's the most important part.

She remembers how silver moonlight bubbled up from the cracks in the sidewalk, pulling Andrew down and holding him once he fell. After a long time clouds moved in and the moon disappeared, but by that time, Andrew was gone.

Elizabeth's parents keep telling her Andrew is dead. They don't remember what really happened, but Elizabeth does. That's why she draws the pictures—to make sure she doesn't forget. She knows that Andrew didn't really die.

The moon stole him away. And that's another thing entirely.

*Who says cats have only nine lives!*

# THE CAT CAME BACK

## Lawrence Watt-Evans

Michael's throat felt tight and heavy, and he tried to swallow but couldn't quite manage it. His eyes were wet with tears as his father lowered the cardboard box into the hole by the back fence.

His two younger sisters were crying and not trying to hide it, but Michael was eleven and he didn't want to cry like a little kid. He kept his mouth tightly closed.

He still couldn't stop a couple of drops from rolling down his cheeks.

"Good-bye, Bootsie," Ashley said. "You were a good cat."

Michael wasn't sure about that, really. He had liked Bootsie, and the cat had been a part of the family, but he wasn't sure he would have called Bootsie a *good* cat. Right up to the end, Bootsie had sometimes mistaken people's legs for scratching posts; he had ruined expensive furniture, knocked glassware off shelves, and left dead squirrels and chipmunks on the front porch.

But he had also been a big, friendly cat, with a purr you could hear clear across the family room. He was always ready to curl up on your lap and be petted. His fur was soft and sleek, and stroking it felt wonderful. He was black, with white feet and a white patch on his face, and could look elegant and noble when he wanted to.

"That was one reason we originally named him after an emperor," their mother had mentioned once, when Michael had commented on how regal Bootsie looked.

"You mean his name wasn't always Bootsie?" Michael had asked, startled.

"No," his mother had said, "we translated it from Latin to English when you were little, because you couldn't pronounce Caligula. Caligula is Latin for Bootsie."

"There was a Roman emperor called Bootsie?" Michael had asked.

His mother had nodded. "One of the very worst," she told him. "And that was another reason we named him that—when he was a kitten, he was the worst nuisance I ever saw. A real little monster."

Michael could believe it—but he couldn't

remember it. Bootsie had been a full-grown cat by the time Michael was born.

And now he was dead.

It wasn't all that surprising for a thirteen-year-old cat to die, but Bootsie hadn't even been sick. He'd just slowed down enough that, after years of trying, Brutus, the dog next door, had finally caught him.

Brutus was supposed to be kept chained up in the backyard, but he got loose fairly often and terrorized all the cats in the neighborhood.

The cats had good reason to be frightened. Michael swallowed again at the memory of finding poor Bootsie dead on the lawn with the dog still standing over him.

Michael's father straightened and picked up the shovel.

For a moment they all stood, not moving, not saying anything. Then, with a sigh, their father started filling in the hole, and Michael and the girls shuffled away, drying their tears.

It was going to be strange not having Bootsie around.

Well, Michael corrected himself, maybe it wouldn't be *that* strange. After all, Bootsie had wandered off a few times.

But he had always come back after a few days, his tail held high and the tip waving back and forth.

This time he wouldn't be coming back.

\*     \*     \*

Michael lay awake in bed that night until almost midnight, staring at the ceiling. He was tired, but he couldn't get to sleep. The wind was blowing hard, rustling the trees and groaning around the eaves, and he kept thinking he heard Bootsie out there, meowing to be let in.

At last, he fell asleep.

He slept late the next day; school wouldn't start for another week, but the summer activities program had ended the previous Friday, so there was no reason to get up at any particular time.

He was still eating breakfast when the doorbell rang. His mother answered it and talked quietly to whoever was there. Michael poked at his cereal, thinking about Bootsie, and paid no attention to anything else until he heard his name called. He looked up. His mother was standing in the doorway.

"What?" he asked.

"I said, have you seen the Marstons' dog this morning?"

"No," Michael said. "Why?"

"Mrs. Marston says he's missing." She turned away again.

Michael resisted the temptation to say, "Good."

A moment later his mother closed the door and said, "When they got up this morning, the doghouse out back was empty, but they just thought he'd gotten out again."

"The way he did when he killed Bootsie," Michael said.

"Yes," his mother answered. "And they thought he would come home again after a couple of hours, but he hasn't turned up yet, and they're getting worried."

"I haven't seen him," Michael said. He turned back to his cereal, hoping that the dog was gone for good.

"He'll probably turn up soon," his mother said. "I hope he doesn't hurt any other cats."

That last comment made Michael feel guilty about not wanting Brutus to come home. He didn't care about the stupid old dog, especially after what he did to Bootsie, but Michael didn't want any other cats to be hurt.

He finished his breakfast and wandered outside with no real plans. He sort of hoped he would find Brutus somewhere, so he could stop worrying about the other neighborhood cats, but he had no idea where to look. He peered up the street, and down, and didn't see any dogs.

He noticed the spot on the front lawn where Bootsie had died—the grass was a bit torn up. His throat tightened. He turned away and walked off, not really thinking about where he was going.

The next thing he knew he was in the backyard, walking toward Bootsie's grave.

It was easy to spot where the cat had been buried; Michael's father had tried to get the grass back in place, but hadn't quite managed it, and a lot of loose brown dirt had been left scattered around the site.

This morning, though, it seemed even messier than it had the day before, and he went to take a closer look.

There was more of a hump than there should be. Michael remembered his father smoothing it down, but now there was a big bulge in the lawn. And the sod was partly rolled back.

Something had been digging there.

Michael felt a hot anger boiling up inside him as he realized what must have happened. Brutus had come over here to dig at Bootsie's grave! Even after Bootsie was dead, that horrible dog wouldn't leave him alone.

Michael was furious as he ran the rest of the way to the grave. He pulled up the strip of sod and tried to straighten it.

Then he glanced down and dropped the sod.

He stared for a moment, then ran back inside to get his mother.

She came to look; so did Mrs. Marston.

But it wasn't until Michael's father got

home that night that anyone touched the grave again.

Michael's mother had explained what happened, how Michael had found Brutus dead under the strip of sod.

"He must have been digging there, and the hole fell in on him," she said, not really sounding as if she believed it.

Michael's father looked puzzled. "I don't see how that could kill him," he said.

But he got the shovel, and everyone went out into the backyard to see.

Michael's father lifted away the sod, then used the shovel to dig away the dirt on either side and uncover Brutus's body. Then he reached down to pick up the dead dog.

He heaved, but the body didn't move, and Michael's father blinked in surprise. "Something's holding him," he said. "He must have gotten trapped somehow, and smothered."

He let go of the dog and cleared away more earth. Michael heard cardboard tearing—the dog must have gotten down as far as the box Bootsie was buried in. He shuddered at the thought.

Michael's father picked the limp dog up again, but something was dangling from its neck.

Then his father lifted the dog higher, and everyone could see what had caught and held

Brutus, what had killed him. Michael's eyes widened with shock.

Bootsie's dead body hung from the dog's throat. The cat's teeth were locked in Brutus's neck, and the dog's blood was smeared on Bootsie's fur.

*This story proves what many of Joe Lansdale's friends have long suspected: The man has one of the weirdest minds in America.*

# THE FAT MAN

## Joe R. Lansdale

The Fat Man sat on his porch in his squeaking swing and looked out at late October. Leaves coasted from the trees that grew on either side of the walk, coasted down and scraped the concrete with a dry, husking sound.

He sat there in his swing, pushing one small foot against the porch, making the swing go back and forth; sat there in his faded khaki pants, barefoot, shirtless, his belly hanging way out over his belt, drooping toward his knees.

And just below his belly button, off-center right, was the tattoo. A half-moon, lying on its back, the ends pointing up. A blue tattoo. An obscene tattoo, made obscene by the sagging flesh on which it was sculpted. Flesh that made the Fat Man look like a hippo if a hippo could stand on its hind legs or sit in a swing pushing itself back and forth.

The Fat Man.

Late October.

Cool wind.

Falling leaves.

The Fat Man with a half-moon tattoo off-center beneath his navel.

The Fat Man swinging.

Everyone wondered about the Fat Man. He had lived in the little house at the end of Crowler Street for a long time. Forever it seemed. As long as that house had been there (circa 1920), he had been there. No one knew anything else about him. He did not go to town. He did not venture any farther than his front porch, as if his house were an oddball ship adrift forever on an endless sea. He had a phone, but no electric lights. He did use gas and he had no car.

And everyone wondered about the Fat Man.

Did he pay taxes?

Where did he get the money that bought the countless boxes of chicken, pizza, egg foo yung and hamburgers he ordered by phone; the countless grease-stained boxes that filled the garbage cans he set off the edge of his porch each Tuesday and Thursday for the sanitation men to pick up and empty?

## The Fat Man

Why didn't he use electric lights?

Why didn't he go to town?

Why did he sit on his porch in his front porch swing looking out at the world, smiling dumbly, going in the house only when night came?

And what did he do at night behind those closed doors?

Why did he wear neither shirt nor shoes, summer or dead of winter?

And where in the world—and why—did he get that ugly half-moon tattooed on his stomach?

Whys and whats. Lots of them about the Fat Man. Questions aplenty, answers none.

Everyone wondered about the Fat Man.

But no one wondered as much as Harold and Joe, two boys who filled their days with comics, creek beds, climbing apple trees, going to school . . . and wondering about the Fat Man.

So one cool night, late October, they crept up to the Fat Man's house, crawling on hands and knees through the not-yet-dead weeds in the empty lot next to the Fat Man's house, and finally through the equally high weeds in the Fat Man's yard.

They lay in the cool, wind-rustled weeds beneath one of the Fat Man's windows and whispered to each other.

"Let's forget it," Harold said.

"Can't. We come this far, and we swore on a dead cat."

"A dead cat don't care."

"A dead cat's sacred, you know that."

"We made that up."

"And because we did that makes it true. A dead cat's sacred."

Harold could not find it in his heart to refute this. They had found the dead cat in the street next to the curb the day before, and Joe had said right off that it was sacred. And Harold, without contesting, had agreed.

And how could he disagree? The looks of the cat were hypnotizing. Its little gray body was worm-worked. Its teeth exposed. Its lips were drawn back, black and stiff. All the stuff to draw the eye. All the stuff that made it sacred.

They took the cat over the creek, through the woods and out to the old "Indian" graveyard and placed it on the ground where Joe said an old Caddo Chief was buried. They took the cat and poked its stiff legs into the soft dirt so that it appeared to be running through quicksand.

Joe said, "I pronounce you a sacred cat with powers as long as there's hair on your body and you don't fall over, whichever comes first."

They made an oath on the sacred cat, and

the oath was this: They were going to sneak over to the Fat Man's house when their parents were asleep, and find out just what in hell and heaven the Fat Man did. Maybe see him eat so they could find out how quickly he went through those boxes and cartons of chicken, pizza, egg foo yung, hamburgers and the like.

Above them candlelight flickered through the thin curtains and window. Joe raised up cautiously for a peek.

Inside he saw the candle residing in a broken dish on an end table next to the telephone. And that was it for the Fat Man's furniture. The rest of the room was filled with food boxes and cartons, and wading knee-deep in their midst was the Fat Man.

The Fat Man had two large trash cans next to him, and he was bending quite nimbly for a man his size (and as he bent the fat about his middle made three thick anaconda coils, one of which was spotted with the blue, half-moon tattoo), picking up the boxes and tossing them in the cans.

Harold raised up for a look.

Soon the cans were stuffed and overflowing and the Fat Man had cleared a space on the floor. With the handle of a can in either hand, the Fat Man swung the cans toward the door, outside and off the edge of the porch.

The Fat Man came back, closed the door, kicked his way through the containers until he reached the clearing he had made.

He said in a voice that seemed somewhat distant, and originating at the pit of his stomach, "Tip, tap, tip tap." Then his voice turned musical and he began to sing "Tip, tap, tip tap."

His bare feet flashed out on the hardwood floor with a sound not unlike tap shoes or wood clicking against wood, and the Fat Man kept repeating the line, dancing around and around, moving light as a ninety-pound ballerina, the obscene belly swinging left and right to the rhythm of his song and his fast-moving feet.

"Tip, tap, tip tap."

There was a knock at the door.

The Fat Man stopped dancing, started kicking the boxes aside, making his way to answer the knock.

Joe dropped from the window and edged around to the corner of the house and looked at the porch.

A delivery boy stood there with five boxes of pizza stacked neatly on one palm. It was that weird guy from Calo's Pizza. The one with all the personality of a puppet. Or at least that was the way he was these days. Once he had been sort of a joker, but the repetition of pizza to go had choked out and hardened any fun that might have been in him.

The Fat Man's hand came out and took the pizzas. No money was exchanged. The delivery boy went down the steps, clicked down the walk, got in the Volkswagen with Calo's Pizza written on the side, and drove off.

Joe crept back to the window, raised up next to Harold.

The Fat Man put the pizza boxes on the end table by the phone, opened the top one and took out the pizza, held it balanced on his palm like a droopy painter's palette.

"Tip, tap, tip tap," he sang from somewhere down in his abdomen, then he turned, his back to the window. With a sudden movement, he slammed the pizza into his stomach.

"Ahhh," said the Fat Man, and little odd muscles like toy trucks drove up and down his back. His khaki-covered butt perked up and he began to rock on his toes. Fragments of pizza, gooey cheese, sticky sauce and rounds of pepperoni dripped to the floor.

The Fat Man's hand floated out, clutched another box and ripped it open. Out came a pizza, wham, into the stomach, "Ah," went the Fat Man, and down dripped more pizza ingredients, and out went the Fat Man's hand once again.

Three pizzas in the stomach.

Now four.

"I don't think I understand all I know about this," Joe whispered.

Five pizzas, and a big "ahhhhhh" this time.

The Fat Man leaped, high and pretty, hands extended for a dive, and without a sound he disappeared into the food-stained cartons.

Joe blinked.

Harold blinked.

The Fat Man surfaced. His back humped up first like a rising porpoise, then disappeared. Loops of back popped through the boxes at regular intervals until he reached the far wall.

The Fat Man stood up, bursting cartons around him like scales. He touched the wall with his palm. The wall swung open. Joe and Harold could see light in there and the top of a stairway.

The Fat Man stepped on the stairway, went down. The door closed.

Joe and Harold looked at each other.

"That wall ain't even a foot thick," Harold said. "He can't do that."

"He did," Joe said. "He went right into that wall and down, and you know it because we saw him."

"I think I'll go home now," Harold said.

"You kidding?"

"No, I ain't kidding."

The far wall opened again and out popped the Fat Man, belly greased and stained with pizza.

Joe and Harold watched attentively as he leaped into the boxes, and swam for the clearing. Then, once there, he rose and put a thumb to the candle and put out the light.

He kicked his way through boxes and cartons this time, and his shadowy shape disappeared from the room and into another.

"I'm going to see how he went through that wall," Joe said.

Joe put his hands on the window and pushed. It wasn't locked. It slid up a few inches.

"Don't," Harold whispered, putting his hand on Joe's arm.

"I swore on the dead cat I was going to find out about the Fat Man, and that's what I'm going to do."

Joe shrugged Harold's arm off, pushed the window up higher and climbed through.

Harold cursed, but followed.

They went as quietly as they could through the boxes and cartons until they reached the clearing where the pizza glop lay pooled and heaped on the floor. Then they entered the bigger stack of boxes, waded toward the wall. And though they went silently as possible, the cartons still crackled and popped, as if they were trying to call for their master, the Fat Man.

Joe touched the wall with his palm the way the Fat Man had. The wall opened. Joe and Harold crowded against each other and looked down the stairway. It led to a well-lit room below.

Joe went down.

Harold started to say something, knew it was useless. Instead he followed down the stairs.

At the bottom they stood awestruck. It was a workshop of sorts. Tubes and dials stuck out of the walls. Rods of glass were filled with pulsating, colored lights. Cables hung on pegs. And there was something else hanging on pegs.

Huge marionettes.

And though they were featureless, hairless and sexless, they looked in form as real as living, breathing people. In fact, put clothes and a face on them and you wouldn't know the difference. Provided they could move and talk, of course.

Harold took hold of the leg of one of the bodies. It felt like wood, but it bent easily. He tied the leg in a knot.

Joe found a table with something heaped on it and covered with black cloth. He whipped off the cloth and said, "Good gracious."

Harold looked.

It was a row of jars, and in the jars, drooping over little upright rods, were masks. Masks of people they knew.

Why, there was Alice Dunn the Avon Lady. They'd know that wart on her nose anywhere. It fit the grumpy personality she had these days.

Jerry James the constable. And my, didn't the eyes in his mask look just like his eyes? The way he always looked at them like he was ready to pull his gun and put them under arrest.

May Bloom, the town librarian, who had grown so foul in her old age. No longer willing to help the boys find new versions of King Arthur or order the rest of Edgar Rice Burroughs' Mars series.

And there was the face of the weird guy from Calo's Pizza, Jake was his name. . . .

"Now wait a minute," Joe said. "All these people have got something in common. What is it?"

"They're grumps," Harold said.

"Uh huh. What else?"

"I don't know."

"They weren't always grumpy."

"Well, yeah," Harold said.

And Harold thought of how Jake used to kid with him at the pizza place. How the constable had helped him get his kite down from a tree. How Mrs. Bloom had introduced him to Edgar Rice Burroughs, Max Brand and King Arthur. How Alice Dunn used to make her rounds, and come back special with a gift for him when he was sick.

"There's another thing," Joe said. "Alice Dunn, the Avon Lady. She always goes door-to-door, right? So she had to come to the Fat Man's door sometime. And the constable, I bet he came, too, on account of all the weird rumors about the Fat Man. Jake, the delivery boy. Mrs. Bloom, who sometimes drives the bookmobile . . ."

"What are you saying?"

"I'm saying that that little liquid in the bottom of each of these jars looks like blood. I think the Fat Man skinned them, and . . ." Joe looked toward the puppets on the wall, "replaced them with handmade versions."

"Puppets come to life?" Harold said.

"Like Pinocchio," Joe said.

Harold looked at the masks in the jars and suddenly they didn't look so much like masks. He looked at the puppets on the wall and thought he recognized the form of one of them; tall and slightly pudgy with a finger missing on the left hand.

"God, Dad," he said.

"He works for Ma Bell," Joe said. "Repairs

lines. And if the Fat Man has phone trouble, and they call out a repairman . . ."

"Don't say it," Harold said.

Joe didn't, but he looked at the row of empty jars behind the row of filled ones.

"What worries me," Joe said, "are the empty jars, and," he turned and pointed to the puppets on the wall, "those two small puppets on the far wall. They look to be about mine and your sizes."

"Oh, they are," said the Fat Man.

Harold shrieked, turned. There at the foot of the stairs stood the Fat Man. And the half-moon tattoo was not a half-moon at all, it was a mouth, and it was speaking to them in the gut-level voice they had heard the Fat Man use to sing.

Joe grabbed up the jar holding Mrs. Bloom's face and tossed it at the Fat Man. The Fat Man swept the jar aside and it crashed to the floor, the mask (face) went skidding along on slivers of broken glass.

"Now that's not nice," said the half-moon tattoo, and this time it opened so wide the boys thought they saw something moving in there. "That's my collection."

Joe grabbed another jar, Jerry James this time, tossed it at the Fat Man as he moved lightly and quickly toward them.

Again the Fat Man swatted it aside, but

now he was chasing them. Around the table they went, around and around like mice pursued by a house cat.

Harold bolted for the stairs, hit the bottom step, started taking them two at a time.

Joe hit the bottom step.

And the Fat Man grabbed him by the collar.

"Boys, boys," said the mouth in the Fat Man's stomach. "Here now, boys, let's have a little fun."

"Run," yelled Joe. "Get help. He's got me good."

The Fat Man took Joe by the head and stuffed the head into his stomach. The mouth slobbered around Joe's neck.

Harold stood at the top of the stairs dumbfounded. In went Joe, inch by inch. Now only his legs were kicking.

Harold slapped his palm along the wall.

Nothing happened.

Up the stairs came the Fat Man.

Harold glanced back. Only one leg stuck out of the belly now, and it was thrashing. The tennis shoe flew off and slapped against the stairs. Harold could hear a loud gurgling sound coming from the Fat Man's stomach, and a voice saying, "ahhhh, ahhhh."

Halfway up the steps came the Fat Man.

Harold palmed the wall, inch by inch.

Nothing happened.

He jerked a glance back again.

There was a burping sound, and the Fat Man's mouth opened wide and out flopped Joe's face, skinned, mask-looking. Harold could also see two large cables inside the Fat Man's mouth. The cables rolled. The mouth closed. Taloned, skinny hands stuck out of the blue tattoo and the fingers wriggled. "Come to Papa," said the voice in the Fat Man's stomach.

Harold turned, slapped his palm on the wall time and again, left and right.

He could hear the Fat Man's tread on the steps right behind him, taking it torturously slow and easy.

The wall opened.

Harold dove into the boxes and cartons and disappeared beneath them.

The Fat Man leaped high, his dive perfect, his toes wriggling like stubby, greedy fingers.

Poof, into the boxes.

Harold came up running, kicking boxes aside.

The Fat Man's back, like the fin of a shark, popped the boxes up. Then he was gone again.

Harold made the clearing in the floor. The house seemed to be rocking. He turned left toward the door and jerked it open.

Stepping out on the front porch he froze.

The Fat Man's swing dangled like an empty canary perch, and the night . . . was different.

Thick as chocolate pudding. And the weeds didn't look the same. They looked like a foamy green sea—putrid sherbet—and the house bobbed as if it were a cork on the ocean.

Behind Harold the screen door opened. "There you are, you bad boy, you," said the voice in the belly.

Harold ran and leaped off the porch into the thick, high weeds, made his way on hands and knees, going almost as fast as a running dog that way. The ground beneath him bucked and rolled.

Behind him he heard something hit the weeds, but he did not look back. He kept running on hands and knees for a distance, then he rose to his feet, elbows flying, strides deepening, parting the waist-level foliage like a knife through spoiled cream cheese.

And the grass in front of him opened up. A white face floated into view at belt-level.

The Fat Man. On hands and knees.

The Fat Man smiled. Skinny, taloned hands stuck out of the blue tattoo and the fingers wiggled.

"Pee-pie," said the Fat Man's belly.

Harold wheeled to the left, tore through the tall weeds, yelling. He could see the moon floating in the sky and it looked pale and sick, like a yolkless egg. The houses outlined across the street were in the right place, but they looked off-key, only vaguely reminiscent of how he remembered them. He thought he saw something large and shadowy peek over the top of one of them, but in a blinking of an eye it was gone.

Suddenly the Fat Man was in front of him again.

Harold skidded to a halt.

"You swore on a dead cat," the voice in the belly said, and a little, wizened, oily head with bugged-out eyes poked out of the belly and looked up at Harold through two sets of arms and smiled with lots and lots of teeth.

"You swore on a dead cat," the voice repeated, only this time it was a perfect mockery of Joe.

Then, with a motion so quick Harold did not see it, the Fat Man grabbed him.

*Poor Jimmy! His parents have dragged him to a new town. His bedroom overlooks the cemetery. And something very weird is coming to visit him tonight.*

# THE HAND

## Eugene M. Gagliano

"The old man's hand got cut off," Richard said, staring at his ten-year-old brother.

"It did not. You're just trying to scare me," Jimmy said, biting his lip.

"And the police never found it, either. Everyone at the high school says the old man looks for it when the moon is full."

"But Mom said the old man who used to live in our house is dead."

Richard grinned. "He is. You sleep in the room that used to be his!"

Goose bumps shot up Jimmy's arms. He looked out the window of their new home in the country. Old Man Baxter was buried in the Kentorville Cemetery just across the road. During the daylight hours it looked quiet and peaceful, but at night he heard strange sounds coming from beyond the fence. His father had told him not to worry. Lots of strange noises could be heard in the country at night. He would get used to it.

Jimmy pushed his hair away from his face. Richard always tried to scare him. He'd get even with his brother someday.

"The guys at school told me the old man died right out there in the field by the barn," Richard taunted. "Maybe some night he'll come looking for his hand. Maybe he'll come up to your room and—"

"Shut up, Richard!"

Jimmy ran up the stairs to his bedroom and slammed the door. He couldn't listen anymore. He might be in the fifth grade, but he was still afraid of the dark. The idea of a ghost looking for a hand in his house scared him. Why did his parents move to this old house anyway? Why did he have to be able to see the cemetery from his bedroom window?

That night, after Jimmy crawled into bed, he remembered what his brother had told him. The moon was full. What if the old man came looking for his hand? What would he do? Jimmy rolled over on his side. "I'm not afraid," he whispered to himself.

\* \* \*

# The Hand

When Jimmy awoke, the moonlight shone on his face. After his eyes adjusted to the light he saw a hand floating inches away from his throat.

The chalky white hand with the bloody wrist lay still. Then it twitched. Jimmy wanted to scream out, but an invisible web of fear stopped him. It wasn't the old man he should have been worried about; it was the old man's hand! He could feel the sweat running down his face. His heart raced in terror. The hand was *alive*.

It floated over to the window, then beckoned him to follow. Jimmy couldn't move. The hand continued to beckon, but when Jimmy did not follow, the hand disappeared from sight. It took hours for Jimmy to fall back to sleep. What if the hand came back? What would he do?

The next morning Jimmy overslept and ended up racing to school. In class he couldn't think about anything but the hand. At recess he decided to ask his new teacher, Ms. Crenshaw, about the old man who used to live in his new house.

"Poor old Mr. Baxter," Ms. Crenshaw said. "He was such a kind and caring man. He lost his wife about a year before the farm accident.

The Baxters had been married for almost fifty years. He never did get over losing her."

*If he was so kind,* Jimmy thought, *then why is he trying to scare the heck out of me?*

"How's my favorite little brother?" Richard asked, coming in from football practice.

"What do you care?"

"My, aren't we touchy? What's the matter? Having a hard time sleeping in the old man's room?"

"Leave me alone!" Jimmy said, slamming his math book closed.

That night when Jimmy went to sleep he left the light on. He woke in the middle of the night. His mother had turned off the light. Moonlight shone in his eyes. That's when he saw it.

Next to him lay the hand again, still and pasty white. It jerked and the skinny fingers motioned him to follow. Jimmy froze. He couldn't breathe. What did it want?

Maybe he was dreaming. Maybe Richard had just scared him too much. Maybe if he closed his eyes it would go away. Jimmy scrunched his eyes tight for a moment, but when he opened them the hand still motioned him to follow.

Jimmy watched as the hand floated out the open window and into the night. It stopped and beckoned him again. Blood dripped from its wrist. Something inside Jimmy told him he had to follow this time. Frightened, but a little curious now, too, he slipped into his jeans and tennis shoes, then tiptoed downstairs and out the door. He followed the hand through the chill night air toward the barn.

A rusty old tractor and a thresher stood next to a mound of rotting hay. The hand hovered over the mound, its shaky white index finger pointing down. Something very important must be in the hay, Jimmy thought to himself. The hand wanted him to find something. But what? And why?

Jimmy searched the hay, but even with the full moon it was too dark to see. Besides, he didn't know what he was looking for.

A dog began to howl mournfully from the direction of the cemetery. The hand suddenly vanished. Jimmy stood alone in the moonlight, goose bumps raising the hair on the back of his neck. He ran back to the house. He'd search the hay mound some more tomorrow.

Jimmy got up early the next morning. He had to tell someone about what happened during the night. But who? If he told Richard, his brother would only tease him about his imagination. If he told his parents, they would think he had had a bad dream. If only his best friend,

Curt, were here instead of 500 miles away in New Jersey.

"Honey, are you all right?" his mother asked at breakfast. "You look tired. Didn't you sleep well?"

"Yeah, what's the matter, Jimmy?" Richard taunted.

"Richard, have you been trying to scare your brother again?" his mother asked. "I wish you would act your age."

"Oh, Mom. Jimmy's not a baby anymore."

"That's right," Jimmy said, flinging a spoonful of granola at his brother.

"Mom, did you see that?" Richard yelled.

"Jimmy, I'm surprised at you. Now apologize and clean up that mess."

"What's the matter? Lose control of your *hand*?" Richard teased.

When Jimmy returned home from school that day, he raced past his mother and up to his room. He stared at his bed. There was no sign of the hand.

Then he got a pitchfork out of the barn and went out to the hay mound. The musty-smelling hay made white puffs of dust as he pulled it apart. Jimmy worked away at it until he saw a glint of light. He stopped and bent to get a closer look. Something gold and shiny lay hidden in the hay. He picked it up and brushed away the dust. It was a gold ring. This must be what the hand wanted. It must be the old man's wedding ring. Jimmy studied the circle of gold in the sunlight, then carefully pushed it deep into his jeans pocket and raced back to the house.

It was hot when Jimmy went to bed that night. He didn't want to leave the window open, but he felt like a baked potato. He looked out at the cemetery. This time he expected the hand to come. The gravestones shimmered in the September moonlight. He could hear strange hooting and chirping sounds. Night in the country was scarier than in the city. He missed the familiar wailing of sirens and the roaring of jets coming in and out of the airport.

Jimmy slid under the covers. The sheets felt cool. He stretched his feet and felt something at the bottom of the bed. It was cold and soft. It felt like—

Jimmy jumped out of bed. He flung the sheet back. The hand, white and wrinkled, slowly dragged itself up the bed toward the pillow. The gnarled fingers motioned Jimmy toward it.

Jimmy knew the hand wanted the ring. It didn't seem to want anything else from him. He took the gold band from where he'd put it on his nightstand and tossed it onto the bed.

The hand crawled over to the ring, then rose into the air and hovered there, trembling.

"What more do you want?" Jimmy whispered. "I got you your ring!"

Jimmy stood motionless for what felt like forever. Did the hand want him to put the ring on its finger? What a creepy thought. Could he do it?

Jimmy bit his lip and stepped forward. He reached toward the ring. He grabbed it and before he could change his mind, pushed it over the bent ring finger of the old man's hand. The hand stopped trembling. For a moment it didn't move. Then it drifted toward Jimmy, gave him a gentle pat on the head, and disappeared.

Jimmy shuddered and crept back into bed. He gave a deep sigh. It was over. Now maybe he could get some sleep; and maybe the old man could, too. His own hand brushed against something wet. He turned on the light by his bed. Blood was spattered across his sheet and pillow. That was all that was left of the hand.

"Good morning, Mom. Good morning, Richard," Jimmy said cheerfully as he entered the kitchen for breakfast.

"How come you're in such a good mood?" his mother asked.

"I'm not afraid of the dark anymore."

"You're not?" Richard asked, sounding almost disappointed. "How come?"

Jimmy smiled. "I guess sometimes you just have to take matters into your own hands."

*Be very careful when you answer the telephone. . . .*

# TOLL CALL

## Michael Mansfield

I know now that there are immortals among us. Today I learned their secret. The telephone rang, and a young man's voice asked, "May I have ten minutes of your time?"

"Sure."

"Thank you," said the voice. The phone clicked in my ear.

Suddenly, I felt just a little older.

*For the third time in this series of anthologies, Michael Markiewicz takes us back to the time when King Arthur was a boy—a time when the only one who knew the boy was going to become king was Merlin the Magician. But with Merlin for a teacher, can magic, danger, and adventure be far behind?*

# MASTER OF THE HUNT

## Michael Markiewicz

We were trapped. Merlin, Arthur, and I had been chased into a dead end with no chance of escape. Now we turned and waited for the horror to bounce around the corner. The thing was worse than a dragon. It was worse than a banshee with a bad attitude. It was crazy Nessie Crackman, a three-hundred-pound lovesick fortune-teller.

Nessie was a wisewoman, of sorts, and said she could tell your future. She was usually wrong, but she made it sound good with a lot of weird moaning and spooky jabber. She said she wanted to learn Merlin's spells, but all she really wanted was a husband. Unfortunately, Nessie was not what you would call a looker—unless you like warts and a hairy lip.

"I've got to get out of here," whispered Merlin as he rummaged through several pouches that hung from his belt.

"Why don't you just talk to her?" asked my little brother, Arthur. He was treading on shaky ground. Telling a wizard what to do was like asking to be turned into a toad. In Arthur's case, I felt that might be an improvement. But I was afraid he'd get us both zapped.

"She's hunting and I'm not about to be snared," rumbled Merlin as he untied a small yellow bag.

My brother didn't understand, but I knew that Nessie had had her eye on Merlin for quite a while. A wizard and a fortune-teller might seem like a natural pair, but Merlin was definitely not the type to settle down—especially with a loon like Nessie.

The sorcerer took a pinch of dust from the bag and tossed it over his head. In a twinkling he disappeared, like a wisp of steam in the cool, late morning air.

"CAI! ARTHUR!" called Nessie as she bobbled into the alley. "I saw that darling man with you. Where has he gone? Merlin! MERLIN!"

"I don't think he's around here," I answered.

"But I saw him!" she whined.

"Um . . ." I thought quickly. "Maybe you should tell us our fortune. If you're right, it might impress Merlin and he'll ask you to show him some of your magic."

I didn't really think she had any magic, but I wanted to make her feel better. I was afraid she might start crying, and that would just be too ugly to bear.

She perked up immediately. "And if I'm right," she answered, "maybe he'll have dinner with me?"

We couldn't guarantee he would do it, but we agreed to ask him.

She grasped our hands with her huge, sweaty palms and stared into space. Suddenly her face twisted into a horrible grimace and she jerked loose violently. With a shaky voice she whispered:

"Fear makes the runner fall,
The faint heart dies too soon,
'Hold firm your ground,' is courage's call,
When horns shall hold the moon."

Her eyes had a wild look and her hair seemed to stand on end. Then she glanced around the alley and beamed a wide smile. "Be sure to tell Merlin about my magic," she exclaimed, and trotted away merrily.

We looked at one another and began to giggle. As the sorceress danced off into the distance, I saw the faint outline of Merlin coming back into focus. He was pouring more dust on his head, this time from a red bag. He stuffed the pouch into a large sack and handed the bundle to Arthur.

"Whew!" exclaimed the wizard. "I can't do that anymore. Especially today. We'd better get out of here and lose that old bat. Let's go hunting."

"Hunting?" I wondered, as Arthur nosed through the contents of the wizard's sack.

"Yes," replied the sorcerer, "today is a great day to go hunting. It's Samhain today and hunting is an old tradition for the holiday."

"But we're supposed to celebrate the harvest festival tonight in the town square," I said.

"Samhain is best celebrated by going on a hunt. It's the night when the Great Hunt gathers the lost souls of this world and takes them to the Netherworld. . . . And if you bag a deer, you can bring it to the feast of Calan Gaeaf tonight at midnight in the town square. Now, doesn't that sound like a great idea?"

It sounded like a lousy idea, but who could tell that to a wizard?

"It's cold," argued Arthur.

"We'll build a fire," parried Merlin.

"And we only have one bow," I offered.

"We'll share," he returned.

"You just want to get away from Nessie Crackman," I said with a smirk.

Merlin muttered something and shook a bony finger in my direction. From his hand came a black puff of smoke.

I didn't like being a slug. First of all, I didn't have any eyes, so I couldn't tell where I was. Second, I was covered in slime. My whole body was one great big white blob of goo. I felt like a living booger.

"Now, shall we go hunting, or shall I get my cat to come out and play with you?" asked the wizard.

I'm not sure if a slug can scream, but I certainly tried.

"Fine," replied Merlin as he puffed me into my human shape. "Then let's get going."

I agreed, but it would have been nice if he had gotten rid of the slime. My pants stuck to my legs and my hair was like a mess of soggy seaweed. It was truly disgusting.

Merlin snatched his bundle from Arthur, then led us out of town and up into the hills. We left the village late that afternoon and made the long trek to the hunting grounds. It was early evening when we finally reached the Cambry Woods. As we walked through the dense trees, Merlin spotted a beautiful stag barely a hundred yards from us.

"Arthur, Cai, come here quickly," he whispered as he knelt behind a large bush.

We crept over and saw through the thick brush a deer with a magnificent rack of antlers. It was calmly feeding on some grass near the edge of a large, open meadow.

"There's your prize, boys," said Merlin as he passed us the bow and motioned toward the animal.

Arthur and I had hunted before, but we had never taken a large animal. Rabbits and squirrels were our usual prey.

"What do we do?" I asked.

"You sneak up on it and shoot it with an arrow," Merlin said sarcastically.

"I know that, but *how*? We can't get across that field without being seen."

"We can do it," said my little brother.

"How?" I asked again, wondering what he was up to.

"Just trust me."

"Good, let's go," ordered Merlin.

"Um . . . couldn't we get it by ourselves?" asked Arthur.

Merlin smiled. "All right. You bag your deer, and I'll meet you over there in that clearing."

Arthur and I crawled through the stand of

thick hardwoods without making a sound. As we crouched under a low bush, my brother showed me why he had wanted to leave Merlin behind. He had taken the sorcerer's yellow pouch with the disappearing dust.

"I snatched it when Merlin gave me his sack," explained my felonious partner.

"He'll turn us both into worms if he finds out you took that," I gasped.

"Not if we come back with that stag's rack on our shoulders!"

In the distance I could hear the sound of wolves baying softly at the setting sun. They had begun their evensong just as Arthur opened the pouch, and I wondered if that was a bad omen.

"That stag will never see us now," he whispered as he took a handful of the magic dust and doused both of us.

At first it tingled. Then it burned a bit. Then I felt as if I was going to be sick. Suddenly the woods looked very different. The plants were all black and the sky was dark gray. There were hardly any colors at all and, worst of all, the wolves sounded much closer. In fact, they seemed to be coming straight for us.

"What happened?" I yelped.

"I don't know," answered Arthur. "Are we invisible?"

"I can't tell," I shouted as the howls became louder.

Everything had changed. It was as if we had slipped through a door into another world. I jumped up and waved my arms at the stag, but the deer looked right through me. Arthur and I could see each other, but we were invisible to everything else.

Then I saw a horrifying sight—hounds with bright white bodies and huge red ears. One of them sniffed the air, looked in our direction, and began to howl wildly. Then a large pack came charging from the woods on the other side of the meadow. Suddenly I realized that it wasn't wolves we had heard, it was the baying dogs of the Hunt. Even though we were invisible, dozens of the grotesque beasts had picked up our scent and were jumping over thickets only a stone's throw away.

Arthur and I ran for our lives as the dogs herded us into the thick woods. We sprinted through tangled branches and hopped two streams, but couldn't lose them. It seemed as if we had been running forever when we finally saw an escape. From a small knoll rose a decrepit old castle with a huge drawbridge. It was so old it was falling in on itself, but it was our only hope. If we could get inside, we might elude the monsters.

We stumbled and scrambled up a gravel

road that led to the abandoned fort. As we reached the bridge, we saw several of the hounds break through the trees. They lunged toward us, but we managed to clear the entrance and drop the portcullis as the beasts reached the top of the hill. The huge metal bars slammed down behind us just in the nick of time.

"What . . . do we do now?" asked Arthur breathlessly.

"First," I panted, "we should use that other dust."

Merlin's disappearing dust clearly hadn't made us invisible to the hounds. In fact, I wondered if that wasn't why they had chased us in the first place.

"That's probably a good idea," answered Arthur, "except—"

"Except? Don't tell me you didn't take the other dust?"

"Sorry."

"The Hunt dogs have decided to eat us for dinner and all you can say is 'Sorry'?"

"Okay, I'm *real* sorry."

"You two will be more than sorry if the Hunt gets you," said a voice from inside the castle's guard tower.

We couldn't see very well into the other room—especially since we were cowering under a large table.

"Who's there?" I asked, peering around one of the dusty wooden legs.

A tall, thin silhouette of a man walked out of the darkened room. Only it wasn't exactly a man. His face was long and pale and his body floated over the ground like a shadow. It was as though he were made of vapor.

"My name is Lord Hardy and I'm the owner of this castle. I'm afraid you can't stay here; this is my haunt. You could haunt the bogs if you wish. Where exactly did you die?"

"D-d-die?" asked Arthur weakly.

My eyes grew as big as saucers as I realized that we were talking to a ghost.

"You are dead, aren't you?" he asked.

Arthur and I stared at the shade in astonishment. Then we inspected each other and realized that we looked just like him. Our bodies had become colorless and transparent, although we didn't seem to float the way he did.

"DEAD?" I screamed at Arthur.

"It couldn't—how could—" stammered my idiot brother.

"I don't believe it. I'm dead," I wailed, "I'm dead! I can't be dead!"

"Well, you can be," answered the ghost. "I am. It's not that bad, really. You get to . . . Um, well, you can, uh . . . Well, yes, it is that bad, I suppose, but there's nothing you can do about it."

Then he looked at us curiously. "Maybe you aren't dead after all," he mused as he studied our misty forms. He curled his finger and beckoned us into another room.

I wasn't sure if I should go along with some specter I hardly knew, but then, what choice did I have? The Hunt dogs were madly thrashing at the main gate, and if we were dead, we had nothing to lose. At least, that's what I thought at the time.

We walked into a great arched room lined with beautiful suits of armor. On the walls were various weapons: swords, lances, maces.

"Hmm," said the ghost, scanning the weapons on the wall. "That's it!" he shouted as he took one of the larger clubs from the collection.

He walked over to us, and without warning, bopped me on the head with the club.

"Oww!" I yelped.

"Oh, good! You're not dead," he replied, and then rapped Arthur sharply.

"Yeoww!" screamed my brother.

"You're not dead, either!"

"Why did you hit us?" I wondered as I rubbed the lump that was growing on my forehead.

"If you were really dead, the club would have passed right through your skull. No knightly weapon is useful against a ghost. . . . But why do you look like ghosts?"

"We used some magic dust from our god-father, Merlin the Wizard," answered Arthur.

*"Today?"*

"Well, yeah. Why not today?" asked my little brother.

"It's Samhain, you fool! Today is the Great Hunt!"

We knew the legend of the Hunt. Gwyn ap Nudd with his white charger and his pack of red-eared hounds gathered the souls of the dead and chased them into the Netherworld on this night. It was a night when both worlds were very close and magic was especially powerful. But we still didn't understand why being invisible was so bad.

The ghost glared at us and shook his head. "You idiots!" he shouted. "In that form, you will be mistaken for dead people by the Hunt and driven into the Netherworld. You'll be stuck there—alive—for all eternity. Trapped forever in a place of death and darkness where you'll never die. You'll feel every minute as though it were time here on Earth. It will be even *worse* than being dead!"

That didn't sound very good. In fact, kissing Nessie Crackman right on her hairy lips sounded better. Not much better, but definitely an improvement.

"Maybe if we hide somewhere the Hunt will leave us alone," I said desperately.

"You can't hide with me. I have a secret passage here in the castle, but only a real ghost could get through the solid rock walls."

Just then we heard a crash. The hounds had broken through the rusty portcullis. We were doomed.

"What are we going to do?" screamed Arthur as we heard the monsters tearing through the castle.

"They've got your scent," said the ghost. "You'll never get away from them. Your only chance is to stand up to the pack."

"Stand up to them?" I cried. "They'll rip us to shreds!"

"Only if you show them you're afraid," he replied. "They're much like ordinary dogs; if you hold your ground, they'll usually respect you."

"Usually?" asked Arthur.

That was my thought exactly. Besides, how can you stand up to something and show that you're not afraid when, in fact, you're completely terrified?

"Don't let them see you shake," he said.

With that, the specter ran straight through one of the walls, leaving us alone in the great hall. We tried to get out the way we came in, but one of the hounds saw us and blocked the door to the courtyard. We had nowhere to go but through a small arrow slit in the outer wall.

Arthur and I squeezed through the narrow opening. It was a twenty-foot drop to the moat. We fell into the green water with a gigantic splash. As the hounds circled back through the castle, we frantically made for shore and then dashed into the woods.

Through the trees we sprinted as fast as our legs would carry us. We gave it our all, but it was impossible to lose the beasts.

Too tired to take another step, we came to a strange-looking field. In the center was a large pit, maybe fifty feet across, and around it were several small boulders. It was so dark we couldn't tell how deep it was. As the hounds closed in on us, Arthur and I huddled against a small rock not far from the pit.

The canine army had charged from the thick, dark forest. Over their ferocious howls we heard a strange trumpet call and then, out of the dust and gloom, appeared a horrifying figure on a gigantic white horse. In his hand was a hunting bugle. Sprouting from his head was an enormous set of antlers. Only one person could look like that: Gwyn ap Nudd, the Master of the Hunt.

As he approached, I could see dozens of

people running in front of him. I started to run with them but Arthur grabbed me from behind.

"What are you doing?" I screamed.

"Look," he answered, pointing to the ominous giant bounding at us.

Gwyn's antlers loomed against the evening sky, and as the moon rose from the trees it shone down directly in the middle of his huge rack. As he came closer, the yellow ball seemed to be cradled over his head like a shining crown.

"Nessie said to hold firm when the moon is held by horns," explained Arthur.

"Nessie?" I blurted. "You're going to listen to her at a time like this?"

"Well, that pit doesn't look like such a good choice."

I looked down, but couldn't see a thing in the enormous hole. It was like a gaping mouth that led to the inside of the earth.

Arthur and I stood shoulder to shoulder and prepared to get mashed into paste by the Master's steed. His brilliant white charger galloped toward us at breakneck speed, and I was sure that if he didn't grind us into a fine powder his dogs would tear us up like rags.

With a tremendous roar the Hunt charged right at us. I braced for the impact as Arthur let out a terrified scream. I even did a little

screaming myself when the crowd ran past us and into the chasm.

In fact, we were so busy screaming that we almost didn't notice what was happening around us. The Master's great steed had nearly run us into the ground when the horned hunter of the dead looked coldly into our eyes and jerked back the reins. He smiled as we clamped our mouths shut and returned his icy stare. Then the gigantic horse suddenly lifted its hooves and leaped into the air. Just as the dogs reached us, they too jumped skyward. The Master's steed flew past our heads and dove into the inky black of the pit. As the horse descended, the pack of baying monsters followed it into the depths.

Arthur and I whirled about and watched them disappear in the blackness. Then, as the moon rose behind us and cast its light into the hole, we noticed a small glimmer far down in the chasm. It was filled with ghosts! This must have been the entrance to the Netherworld and those people were spirits. If we had jumped in, we would have been trapped with them forever. Nessie had been right.

Arthur and I staggered from the forest as fast as our weary legs could carry us. Meeting danger head-on, visiting with local ghosts, and staring into the depths of the Netherworld tend to make one anxious to get home. We managed to run back to the clearing where Merlin was still waiting. But one problem remained: We were still invisible, and the only way to undo it was to go to Merlin and try to get his other pouch.

We crept up on the wizard and tried to lift the sack that contained his magic potions. If we could just sneak it away from him for a minute, we could undo the spell and he would never have to know about our taking it. Arthur reached out for the pouch as Merlin stroked his beard.

"It's about time you boys were back," he said calmly.

"You can see us!" I gasped.

"Wizards can see a lot of things," he replied. "Where have you been?" he asked as he doused both of us with the reappearing dust.

There was no point in lying now. We told the magician the whole tale about the ghost and the Master and how we had narrowly escaped death.

"Merlin," I asked, hoping he wasn't too angry, "before you turn us into worms, could you tell me one thing?"

"Hmm?"

"Why did the Hunt jump over us when we stood there? They could easily have taken us into the Netherworld."

The sorcerer grinned and said, "The Netherworld only welcomes those who flee into its depths of their own choosing. If you have courage, no one, not even the Master, can force you into that place. There are much better places for brave men."

He looked at us carefully and added, "Well, you seem to have learned a great lesson. Always meet your problems head-on and your courage will see you through. I suppose you can just clean out the pigs' trough as a suitable punishment. You can—"

"OH, MERLIN!" croaked a familiar voice as Nessie lumbered toward us from the town road. "I proved I could handle some magic. I told them their fortune and I was right, you know. Would you like to have—"

Merlin was about to dip into his bag and disappear again when Arthur blurted, "Like you said, Merlin, meet your problems head-on. That's just what we're going to do!"

"Right," I chimed. "Stand your ground and your courage will see you through!"

As I said, telling a wizard what to do was a dangerous idea. But in this case, it taught me two important things. First, being a smart aleck is not the same thing as holding onto your courage. Second, being turned into a toad was just as bad as being a slug.

*Few things are more inherently magical than puppets. Put one on your hand, and you can give it a personality of its own. Unless, of course, it already has one. . . .*

# GIVE A PUPPET A HAND

## Mary Downing Hahn

One rainy morning Mom woke me, shaking my shoulder and shouting my name. "Jeremy, what are you still doing in bed? You should be dressed and at the breakfast table. You've already gotten five demerits for tardiness from Miss Wockanfuss. Do you want to fail sixth grade?"

I shook my head. The only thing I really wanted was to pull the covers over my head and tell Mom I was sick, that my throat hurt, my head hurt, my stomach hurt, I was getting a funny rash. . . . But I'd tried all these symptoms already with no success. When your mother works, there's no way to stay home unless you're truly dying.

So I made my usual excuse. "The alarm didn't go off."

Of course, Mom didn't buy that. Without another word, she yanked off my blankets and stamped out of the room, leaving me cold and shivering and feeling sorrier for myself than usual.

Ten minutes later I was sloshing to school through the rain. While I was waiting to cross the street, a passing car sprayed me with muddy water. I jumped back from the curb and dropped my homework in a puddle. Naturally I'd written it in washable ink. By the time I'd fished it out, all my vocabulary words had dissolved into a blue blur. An hour's worth of work down the old drain.

"Well, if isn't Jeremy Germ."

Just ahead, my enemy, Nelson Biggs, blocked the sidewalk, his fat hand held out for me to surrender my lunch money.

"Don't keep me waiting, Germ."

There was no use running, no use fighting. Wordlessly I handed him a dollar bill. Instead of saying thanks, he punched me in the stomach.

"If they have spinach today," he said, "I'll give mine to you."

I hurried the rest of the way and was only one measly minute late for school, but Miss Wockanfuss got mad anyway, probably because she hated me and always had. You've heard of love at first sight? For Miss Wockanfuss and me it was hate at first sight, though I don't think anyone really liked her or she liked anyone else.

"No excuses," she yelled. "In my classroom, punctuality counts!"

Miss Wockanfuss sent me to the cloakroom to think about that.

Not long after she let me out, she got angry all over again at the sight of my soggy, ruined homework. "No excuses!" she hollered at me. "In my classroom, neatness counts."

Miss Wockanfuss sent me back to the cloakroom to think about that.

In the cafeteria, I was the only kid who ate his spinach. As if that wasn't bad enough, Nelson walked by and jiggled my arm, making me spill half of it down the front of my shirt. For the rest of the day I was known as the green germ.

After lunch, Miss Wockanfuss caught me daydreaming. "No excuses!" she shouted. "In my classroom, paying attention counts!"

Back to the cloakroom I went to think about that. I was getting to know my classmates' coats pretty well.

Just before dismissal, Miss Wockanfuss caught me reading a library book when everyone else was doing long division. "No excuses!" she screamed. "In my classroom, reading for fun *doesn't* count!"

This time the cloakroom wasn't enough. Miss Wockanfuss kept me after school. She made me write, "I will be on time, I will be neat, I will pay attention, I will not read in class" 273 times multiplied by 99 and divided by 7.7.

She did not return my library book to me before school ended, adding another five cents to the quarter I already owed on it. Soon the librarian would hate me, too.

Hours later I left school, hungry, unhappy, and misunderstood. As I was passing a dark alley, I heard a funny, squeaky voice say, "Poor Jeremy Miller, oh, poor, poor Jeremy Miller—his day's been a killer!"

I stopped and peered into the shadows. "Who said that?"

A strange face popped up from behind a garbage can. It had beady little eyes, a long red nose, a wide mouth, and a big chin. It wore a jester's cap trimmed with bells. When it nodded its head, the bells jingled merrily. "Jeremy Germ, Jeremy Germ, you're an ugly little worm."

Behind the garbage can was a shabby old man with the saddest face I ever saw. The puppet danced at the end of his arm. "Hello,

sonny," the old man said softly. "How do you like Mr. Punkerino? I bet you never saw a finer puppet. Made of the finest silk and satin and stuffed with pure glee."

The puppet laughed and clapped his hands. "Hooray, hooray," he crowed, "for Mr. Punkerino!"

"How did you know my name?" I asked, not sure who to speak to, the puppet or the old man. They were both staring at me.

"Name shame—who's to blame?" The puppet laughed loudly but the old man didn't even smile. Watching me closely, he stretched out his arm, bringing the puppet nearer and nearer to me.

"I'm Mr. Punkerino," sang the puppet, "a jolly rogue am I! I'll make you laugh, I'll make you glad, I'll be the funniest friend you ever had!"

The old man held the puppet right under my nose. "Mr. Punkerino likes you, Jeremy," he said.

The puppet nodded his head, making the bells on his cap ring. "It would be grand if you'd give me a hand."

Suddenly I wanted that puppet more than anything in the whole world. I just had to have him. Without thinking, I reached for Mr. Punkerino. "Give him to me."

The moment the words left my mouth, a

gust of wind sent a flurry of dead leaves, old papers, and dirt spiraling toward me. In the middle of the whirling dust devil, everything turned dark. Then, as suddenly as it came it was gone. I blinked and opened my eyes.

"Jeremy, Jeremy, now you must carry me."

The old man had vanished and I was amazed to see Mr. Punkerino on my hand, grinning and waving his tiny fists. "You talked," I said. "You must be battery operated."

"Chattery, chattery," he said, "the best things are done without a battery."

The puppet was a tight fit, sort of like a glove a size too small, and he made my hand uncomfortably warm. I grasped his head, thinking I'd pull him off and figure out how he worked, but I couldn't budge him. It was as if he'd grown to my hand. Even though it hurt, I yanked and tugged and twisted till my hand felt like it would fall off. While I struggled, the puppet shrieked, "Stop! Stop! I'll blow my top!"

Finally I gave up and leaned against a wall. For a few seconds, the only sound was my breathing—and his. Yes, Mr. Punkerino was out of breath, too. Worse yet, I could feel his heart beating like a trapped bird's.

Terrified, I stared into the puppet's beady eyes. "What are you?" I whispered.

A crafty grin spread across his face. "I can't say just how, but I'm your best pal now."

Just then a shadow fell across the alley's entrance. Hoping the old man had returned to explain the trick, I whirled around—and saw Nelson Biggs staring at me.

"Playing with dolls, Jeremy? I always knew you were a little strange."

Thrusting Mr. Punkerino behind me, I shook my head. I intended to run, but somehow my feet stayed where they were. "Get lost, you big fat dummy!" I heard myself yell. "You're asking for a sock in the tummy!"

Nelson stared at me in astonishment, but he wasn't any more surprised than I was. Even though the voice sounded exactly like mine, Mr. Punkerino had spoken, not me. I opened my mouth to explain.

"Nelson, Nelson ate my lunch," I found myself saying instead. "Nelson, Nelson, want a punch?"

"Why, you little jerk." Nelson stepped toward me, his face purple with rage, but he never got a chance to hit me. Using my fist, Mr. Punkerino lowered his head and butted Nelson's stomach so hard my hand smarted.

"Oof!" Nelson fell to the ground and stared at me, his eyes wide. "Have you gone nuts?"

"Crazy as a daisy," I said, "loony as the moon."

Nelson backed away. At the end of the alley, he took one last wondering look at me and fled.

"Stinky, stinky Nelson!" Mr. Punkerino shouted at my enemy's back.

"This is all wrong," I whispered to the puppet. "I'm supposed to make you talk, I'm supposed to make you move, but you, you—"

"Puppetry buppetry boo hoo hoo," Mr. Punkerino interrupted. "You've given your hand to a jolly old man."

Once more I grabbed his head and yanked as hard as I could. The puppet fit even tighter than before. I gave up in tears.

"There's nothing you can do," Mr. Punkerino said. "I'm really stuck on you."

Next I tried to jam him into my pocket, but he beat me with his little fists and shrieked, "Take me home, take me home. Never will I roam!"

By the time I climbed the three flights of steps to our apartment, I was so exhausted I wanted to go to bed. Instead I had to face my mother.

"You're late, Jeremy. Did Miss Wockanfuss keep you after school again?"

"She walked, she fussed, she even cussed," sang Mr. Punkerino. "I'm so bad I made her sad."

Mom stared at me. "What did you say?"

Before Mr. Punkerino could say more, I ran down the hall to my room. "I have to do my homework!" I yelled, and slammed the door.

When it was time for dinner, I kept Mr. Punkerino in my lap and tried to eat with my left hand. Mom looked at me, obviously puzzled. "Is something wrong, Jeremy?"

I shook my head. If I didn't open my mouth, maybe Mr. Punkerino couldn't speak. Of course, I underestimated him. Peering over the edge of the table, he waved his little fists at Mom.

Startled by my unusual antics, Mom stared at Mr. Punkerino. "Where did you get that dirty old puppet, Jeremy?"

Mr. Punkerino scowled. "I'm cleaner than you. You smell like a shoe."

"Don't be impudent," Mom said to me. "Take that thing off your hand and eat your dinner." Impatiently she reached out to grab the puppet, but he dodged aside.

"I'm sorry," I said desperately. "We're putting on a play at school. Miss Wockanfuss told us to wear our puppets all day. That way we'll get used to them, they'll feel natural on our hands, they'll seem like they're part of us."

Mr. Punkerino laughed. "Give a puppet a hand," he sang. "You'll soon understand!"

Mom smiled. "You should get an 'A' the

way you bring that puppet to life. I swear his face changes, his eyes twinkle; why, he all but breathes."

The next morning I left for school an hour early, hoping to find the old man in the alley and make him take back the puppet. I was already on Miss Wockanfuss' bad side. What she would do when she saw Mr. Punkerino didn't bear thinking about.

At the entrance to the alley, Mr. Punkerino said, "You can't give me away. I'm yours for many a day."

I ignored him. The old man was going through the trash cans, making so much noise he didn't see me until I was close enough to grab his sleeve.

"No," he whispered, "no, not you."

I didn't know whether he meant me or Mr. Punkerino, but I thrust the puppet at him. "You put this on my hand, now take it off!"

"Fickle, fickle," Mr. Punkerino said, "got a face like a pickle."

The old man shook his head. "Begging your pardon, but nobody can give you what you don't want. You asked for him. You got him."

Before I could say a word, the old man pulled loose and ran, a flash of gray rags disappearing down the alley. By the time I reached Elm Street, there was no sign of him. It looked like I'd have to take Mr. Punkerino to school after all. If he acted up—and I was sure he would—I'd probably spend the rest of my life in the principal's office.

I slid into my seat just as the bell rang. Miss Wockanfuss shot me a nasty look, but she couldn't send me to the cloakroom. For once I wasn't late.

Mr. Punkerino behaved for a while. He stayed on my lap out of sight. Every now and then he sighed, but he didn't speak. Then a folded piece of paper landed at my feet. A note to pass on, I figured. But no—it had my name on it. I opened it cautiously, thinking it might be a death threat from Nelson.

"I hear you socked Nelson Biggs," I read. "I think you're wonderful." It was signed "Violet Rose."

I glanced at her across the room and she smiled so sweetly my heart stopped for a second and then beat so fast I thought it would fly out the window. Violet Rose had never even looked at me before. Could it be she liked me?

"Jeremy!" Miss Wockanfuss thundered. Her bosom swelled, her face turned red, she strode down the aisle, shaking the floor like a brontosaurus on a rampage. "Why are you smiling? No excuses! Happiness is not allowed. Nobody has a good time in my class!"

She was just about to send me to the cloakroom to think about that when Mr. Punkerino said, "Walk and fuss, walk and cuss. You look just like a junkyard bus."

For a moment there was deadly silence. My classmates held their breath. They didn't move, they didn't even blink. Miss Wockanfuss puffed up like a balloon about to explode.

"Jeremy Miller, you go to the principal this moment!" she shouted.

When I stood up to leave, Mr. Punkerino shook his fists and laughed. "You make me ill, you big fat pill."

Violet Rose turned pale. Nelson gasped. The whole class cowered.

Miss Wockanfuss reached for Mr. Punkerino. "Give me that!"

In a flash, the puppet was on Miss Wockanfuss' hand. She stared at Mr. Punkerino, obviously surprised. At that moment, the principal entered the room.

"Miss Wockanfuss," Mr. Dinkerhoff said, "what's going on in here? I can hear the noise all the way down the hall in my office."

Miss Wockanfuss was struggling to remove the puppet, but her efforts didn't stop Mr. Punkerino from saying—in her voice—"What's it to you, Mr. Dinkydoodoo?"

It was Mr. Dinkerhoff's turn to be surprised. "What did you say?"

135

Miss Wockanfuss shook her fist, her face purple, but she couldn't free her hand. No matter what she did, she couldn't silence Mr. Punkerino, either. "I've had it with you, Mr. Dinkydoodoo," he sang. "Go jump in a lake, you silly old fake!"

Mr. Dinkerhoff took Miss Wockanfuss firmly by the arm. Turning to us, he said, "Please excuse your teacher's behavior, boys and girls. She isn't well."

"Quick, quick, I'm sick, I'm sick," cried Mr. Punkerino. "Take me away, call it a day!"

"Yes, yes, dear Emma," Mr. Dinkerhoff said soothingly. "Sit tight, boys and girls. We'll send a substitute as soon as we can."

Still shaking her fist, Miss Wockanfuss left the room. Just before he disappeared with her, Mr. Punkerino waved to me. "So long, goodbye, please don't cry. You won't see me again, I've found a brand-new friend."

For a few moments nobody spoke. Then Violet Rose got to her feet. "Hip hip hooray for Jeremy," she shouted. "Let's give him a great big hand for getting rid of the meanest teacher in the world!"

Everyone clapped, even Nelson. I'd like to say I felt sorry for Miss Wockanfuss, but even when they took her away in a straitjacket, the only sympathy I felt was for Mr. Punkerino. Poor puppet—I bet he didn't know what a bad hand he'd been dealt.

*Some parties are stranger than others.*

# HALLOWEEN PARTY

## Steven Prohaska

I looked in the mirror and was pleased at the image. My bulging yellow eyes glowed against my mottled green skin. Several large brown moles, dark hairs rising from their centers, dotted my face. My mouth was frozen in a grin, revealing twisted yellow teeth with jagged edges.

Beautiful. Simply beautiful.

"Are you almost ready, dear?" my mom called from downstairs.

I reached up, pulled the mask up and over my face, and yelled, "Yeah, Mom. Just give me a few more minutes." I glanced around my room and snatched up a flashlight and my jack-o'-lantern bucket.

"Hurry up, Michael! Your brother is ready to go trick-or-treating!"

I pulled my goblin mask back on and raced

downstairs to see my eight-year-old brother, Eric, in a billowing ghost costume.

Eric moaned in his best ghost imitation. "Boooo!"

I stood still, not reacting.

"You were scared and you know it!" said Eric.

"Goblins don't get scared," I replied in my most chilling, raspy voice. "They scare their victims!" Raising my arms high over my head, I thrust my face close to his.

Eric fell to the rug, and I bent close to his neck as if to bite him. He began to howl just as my mom came into the living room.

"Stop that, Michael," said Mom automatically. Her back was to us and she was pouring candy into a large plastic bowl.

I looked back at Eric. "We'd better get going—on Halloween, time is candy!"

"Remember to be home by nine-thirty," Mom said.

I looked at my watch. It was 6:45. I turned to my brother. "Okay, Eric. Let's trick-or-treat until eight o'clock, then we'll go to Chris's party. Do you know where his house is?"

"Yeah."

I was glad one of us knew. I didn't want to admit I'd forgotten to ask Chris for directions.

We trick-or-treated till about 7:30, but got

mostly ho-hum kinds of candy, like Gummy
Bears and SweeTarts. I had visions of Mars
bars, Baby Ruths, and Snickers bars overflowing my bucket. "Maybe we should split up," I
suggested. I knew some big houses farther
away, where they always gave out great candy.
But my brother would never make it there and
back in time with his short legs.

"Mom said you had to stay with me." He
sounded irritated.

We argued but finally decided to meet back
there at the corner of Twelfth and Oak at 8:00.
Eric nodded and stumped off.

In what seemed like twenty minutes my
bucket was filled with good candy. Starting
back to the meeting place, I glanced at my
watch. To my horror it was 8:15. I was late!

I ran so hard that my sides felt as if they
were going to burst.

Eric was nowhere in sight.

I looked around frantically. The street
lamps cast orange pools of light inside larger
areas of deep shadow. There was a chill in the
air and the wind moaned slightly. Finally, I noticed a white specter about three hundred feet
ahead. Eric . . . I hoped. I hurried after him, but
I couldn't catch up.

"Hey, Eric!" I yelled, running faster.
"Wait!"

He didn't seem to pay any attention, and

in the dim light it looked as if he were flying ahead. I saw the ghost go into a house. That must be where the party was. But as I glanced around, the neighborhood didn't look right. Stunted trees grew everywhere, and only a few patches of dead, withered grass dotted the ground.

I approached the house and walked up to the front door, shivering as I noticed the skull-shaped doorknob. Cobwebs draped each window. These people sure believed in realism.

I was let into the party by a snake-headed creature. The scaled, pale-green skin had a waxy, almost oily sheen. A great costume. I couldn't tell where the mask ended.

"Have you seen my brother, Eric?" I asked.

The creature raised a glass of dark red punch and took a giant swallow.

"He's dressed up as a ghost," I added.

The snake creature looked at me with cold black eyes and laughed. "Dressed up?" it said in a throaty voice. I caught a glimpse of a long, red forked tongue. The creature laughed again and walked away. Confused, I took a glass of punch from a table and looked around the room.

Monsters of every description filled the place: werewolves, mummies, witches, vampires, giant spiders. No ghosts, though. I had never seen such great costumes. One of the werewolves looked as if he was really drooling. I headed upstairs to look for Eric. The risers squeaked with each of my steps. A thick wad of cobwebs got onto my mask. I brushed them away. They didn't look like fake cobwebs at all.

I stopped at the landing. "Eric?" I called. "Hey, Eric, are you up here?"

I lifted my mask slightly, raised the punch glass, took a sip, and spat it out in disgust. It tasted salty and burned my mouth. I looked where I had spat out the liquid: It bubbled and popped; vapor rose from the spot.

This was no costume party.

I ran downstairs, suddenly wanting nothing more than to get out. My heart thudded wildly in my chest. I was almost to the door when a cold hand gripped my shoulder and held me back.

"Where are you going?" an icy voice demanded.

I spun around and came face-to-face with a vampire.

"You know that no monster—once inside—can pass beyond that door on Halloween night."

"I . . . forgot," I stammered, trying to sound like a goblin.

The vampire stared intently for a moment

with his glowing red eyes, sneered, and tore off my mask. All the monsters turned and stared.

A witch stepped forward, shrieking: "A human! A human does not deserve to drink the sacred elixir!" She smashed the glass from my hand, leaving me holding only the stem.

I tucked the broken stem in my pocket as I backed slowly toward the doorway. I glanced over my shoulder—several creatures had moved to block me. All the monsters started forming a rough circle around me.

"We cannot release you," the vampire said calmly. "You will stay with us. . . ."

My end had come. *Try something, try anything*, I thought. "I know that," I growled. "I'm a monster dressed up as a human!" I made a fearsome face and roared. Several monsters started murmuring. I kept my eyes on the vampire, who was looking at me in a calculating way. From the corner of my left eye, I saw a place where the circle of monsters was thinner. Beyond it was the staircase.

"Look over there!" I yelled, pointing to the right. Several of the monsters turned to look. Even the vampire flicked his eyes in that direction. Instantly I saw my chance and bolted to the left. I ducked my head, screaming at the top of my lungs. I plowed straight through the few monsters standing there, knocking them to the floor. They howled in rage behind me as

I raced across the floor and back up the stairs. I shot past the landing and up another flight of stairs. The monsters were now close behind.

I ran into a large bedroom and slammed the door shut, then locked it. Instantly, there was a furious pounding on the door. I grabbed a chair and jammed it between the doorknob and the floor. The pounding grew louder.

Looking over my shoulder, I saw a window on the other side of a giant canopy bed. I ran over and tried to open the window. It was locked. I unlocked it and pulled up, but it still wouldn't move. The window was made of thick leaded-glass panes that looked unbreakable.

*BAM!* The door shuddered, but held.

Getting a better hold on the window, I pulled again. Nothing. It probably hadn't been opened in a hundred years. I pulled again with all my might, huffing with the effort.

*BAM!* The door shuddered again, and sounded as if it had cracked.

Sweat trickled off my brow. I could feel the veins stand out on my neck. With a final burst of energy, I pulled with all my strength. The window slid up with a groan, stopping after about a foot. I pushed the screen out of the frame. Cold rain slapped against my face. I got on the sill and started out the window.

*BAM!* I could hear the chair crack and

break; the door burst open and slammed against the wall.

Squeezing my body through the window, I grasped the drainpipe that ran down the wall. Before I could get completely through the window, sharp talons grabbed my ankles. I heard a howl of savage laughter. I clawed at the pipe and kicked my feet back and forth. My sneakers came off, but the monster lost its hold on my ankles, and I got through the window. I had a death grip on the drainpipe as I began shinnying down.

The drainpipe was old and rusted. I had barely started down when it began to creak and loosen. The small screws that held it to the outside wall popped loose—and the pipe broke away. I let go and fell to the ground. My head crashed against a rock. Darkness overcame me.

The next day I awoke to the sound of birds chirping. Sunshine was streaming into my room through the window by my bed. I was sweating profusely. I realized that I had just had a bad dream.

Eric walked into the room, eating a Mr. Goodbar. "That wasn't very nice of you—leaving me alone last night. Don't worry, though, I haven't told Mom . . . yet. We can work out a payment schedule later. Heh heh. Anyway,

Mom wants to know how you got mud all over the house last night."

Eric left the room, whistling tunelessly. I sat up and swung my legs over the side of the bed. I noticed that I was still wearing my jeans. I felt something in my pocket. A chill went down my back as I reached in and pulled it out.

Lying in the palm of my hand was the broken stem of a punch glass.

*The house in this story is based on the house where Jane Yolen lives. The ritual is one her own children developed when they were little, and the scene where the baby-sitter confronts the principal is based on real life. Everything else, Jane assures me, is made up. . . .*

# THE BABY-SITTER

## Jane Yolen

Hilary hated baby-sitting at the Mitchells' house, though she loved the Mitchell twins. The house was one of those old, creaky Victorian horrors, with a dozen rooms and two sets of stairs. One set led from the front hall and one, which the servants had used back in the 1890s, led up from the kitchen.

There was a long, dark hallway upstairs, and the twins slept at the end of it. Each time Hilary checked on them, she felt as if there were things watching her from behind the closed doors of the other rooms or from the walls. She couldn't say what exactly, just *things*.

"Do this," Adam Mitchell had said to her the first time she'd taken them up to bed. He touched one door with his right hand, the next with his left, spun around twice on his right leg, then kissed his fingers one after another. He repeated this ritual three times down the hall to the room he shared with his brother, Andrew.

*"Once a night,*
*And you're all right,"*

he sang in a Munchkin voice.

Andrew did the same.

Hilary laughed at their antics. They looked so cute, like a pair of six-year-old wizards or pale Michael Jackson clones, she couldn't decide which.

"You do it, Hilary," they urged.

"There's no music, guys," she said. "And I don't dance without music."

"It's not dancing, Hilly," Adam said. "It's magic."

"It keeps *Them* away," Andrew added. "We don't like *Them*. Grandma showed us how. This was her house first. And her grandmother's before her. If you do it, *They* won't bother you."

"Well, don't worry about *Them*," Hilary had said. "Or anything else. That's what I'm hired for, to make sure nothing bad happens to you while your mom and dad are out."

But her promises hadn't satisfied them, and in the end, to keep them happy, she banged on each door and spun around on her right leg, and kissed her fingers, too. It was a lot of fun, actually. She had taught it to her best friend, Brenda, the next day in school, and pretty soon half the kids in the ninth grade had picked it up. They called it the Mitchell March, but secretly Hilary called it the Spell.

The first night's baby-sitting, after they had danced the Spell all the way down the long hall, Hilary had tucked the boys into their beds and pulled up a rocking chair between. Then she told them stories for almost an hour until first Adam and then Andrew fell asleep. In one night she'd become their favorite baby-sitter.

She had told them baby stories that time— "The Three Bears" and "Three Billy Goats Gruff" and "Three Little Pigs," all with sound effects and a different voice for each character. After that, she relied on TV plots and the books she'd read in school for her material. Luckily she was a great reader. The twins hated to ever hear a story a second time. Except for "The Golden Arm," the jump story that she'd learned on a camping trip when she was nine.

Adam and Andrew asked for *that* one every time.

When she had asked them why, Adam had replied solemnly, his green eyes wide, "Because it scares *Them*."

After she smoothed the covers over the sleeping boys, Hilary always drew in a deep breath before heading down the long, uncarpeted hall. It didn't matter which stairs she headed for, there was always a strange echo as she walked along, each footstep articulating with precision, and then a slight tap-tapping afterward. She never failed to turn around after the first few steps. She never saw anything behind her.

The Mitchells called her at least three times a month, and though she always hesitated accepting, she always went. Part of it was she really loved the twins. They were bright, polite, and funny in equal measure. And they were not shy about telling her how much they liked her. But there was something else, too. Hilary was a stubborn girl. You couldn't tell from the set of her jaw; she had a sweet, rounded jaw. And her nose was too snubbed to be taken seriously. But when she thought someone was treating her badly or trying to threaten her, she always dug in and made a fuss.

Like the time the school principal had tried to ban miniskirts and had sent Brenda home for wearing one. Hilary had changed into her junior varsity cheerleading uniform and walked into Mr. Golden's office.

"Do you like our uniforms, sir?" she had said, quietly.

"Of course, Hilary," Mr. Golden had answered, being too sure of himself to know a trap when he was walking into it.

"Well, we represent the school in these uniforms, don't we?" she had asked.

"And you do a wonderful job, too," he said.

*Snap. The sound of the closing trap.* "Well, they are shorter than any miniskirt," she said. "And when we do cartwheels, our bloomers show! Brenda never does cartwheels." She'd smiled then, but there was a deep challenge in her eyes.

Mr. Golden rescinded the ban the next day.

So Hilary didn't like the idea that any *Them*, real or imagined, would make her afraid to sit with her favorite six-year-olds. She always said yes to Mrs. Mitchell in the end.

It was the night before Halloween, a Sunday, the moon hanging ripely over the Mitchells' front yard, that Hilary went to sit for the twins. Dressed as a wolf in a sheep's clothing, Mr. Mitchell let her in.

"I said they could stay up and watch the Disney special," he said. "It's two hours, and well past their bedtime. But we are making an exception tonight. I hope you don't mind." His sheep ears bobbed.

She had no homework and had just finished reading Shirley Jackson's *The Haunting of Hill House*, which was scary enough for her to prefer having the extra company.

"No problem, Mr. Mitchell," she said.

Mrs. Mitchell came out of the kitchen carrying a pumpkin pie. Her costume was a traditional witch's. A black stringy wig covered her blond hair. She had blackened one of her front teeth. The twins trailed behind her, each eating a cookie.

"Now, no more cookies," Mrs. Mitchell said, more to Hilary than to the boys.

Hilary winked at them. Adam grinned, but Andrew, intent on trying to step on the long black hem of his mother's skirt, missed the wink.

"Good-bye," Hilary called, shutting the door behind the Mitchells. She had a glimpse of the moon, which reminded her of the Jackson book, and made a face at it. Then she turned to the twins. "Now, what about those cookies?" she asked.

They raced to the kitchen and each had

one of the fresh-baked chocolate-chip cookies, the kind with the real runny chocolate.

"Crumbs don't count," Hilary said. She scraped around the dish for the crumbs, and having counted what remained—there were thirteen—she shooed the boys back into the living room. They turned on the TV and settled down to watch the show, sharing the handful of crumbs slowly through the opening credits.

Adam lasted through the first hour, but was fast asleep in Hilary's lap before the second. Andrew stayed awake until nearly the end, but his eyes kept closing through the commercials. At the final ad for vitamins, he fell asleep for good.

Hilary sighed. She would have to carry them upstairs to bed. Since she wanted to watch *Friday the Thirteenth, Part II*—or at least she thought she wanted to watch it—she needed to get them upstairs. It wouldn't do for either one to wake up and be scared by the show. And if she woke them, they'd want to know the end of the Disney movie and hear at least one other story. She would miss her show. So she hoisted Adam in her arms and went up the stairs.

He nuzzled against her shoulder and looked so vulnerable and sweet as she walked down the creaky hall, she smiled. Playfully, she touched the doors in the proper order, turning around heavily on one leg. She couldn't quite reach her fingers until she dumped him on his bed. After covering him with his quilt, she kissed his forehead and then, with a grin, kissed each of her fingers in turn, whispering, "So there" to the walls when she was done.

She ran down the stairs for Andrew and carried him up as well. He opened his eyes just before they reached the top step.

"Don't forget," he whispered. To placate him, she touched the doors, turned, and kissed her fingers one at a time.

He smiled sleepily and murmured, "All right. All right now."

He was fast asleep when she put him under the covers. She straightened up, watched them both for a moment more, listened to their quiet breathing, and went out of the room.

As she went down the stairs, the hollow tap-tapping echo behind her had a furtive sound. She turned quickly, but saw nothing. Still, she was happy to be downstairs again.

The first half of the show was scary enough. Hilary sat with her feet tucked under a blanket, arms wrapped around her legs. She liked scary stuff usually. She had seen *Alien* and *Aliens* and even *Jaws* without blanching, and had finished a giant box of popcorn with Brenda at the *Night of the Living Dead*. But somehow, watching a scary movie alone in the

Mitchells' spooky house was too much. Remembering the popcorn, she thought that eating might help. There were still those thirteen chocolate-chip cookies left. Mrs. Mitchell meant the boys weren't supposed to eat them. Hilary knew she hadn't meant the baby-sitter to starve.

During the commercials, she threw off the blanket and padded into the kitchen. Mrs. Mitchell had just had new linoleum put on the floor. With a little run, Hilary slid halfway across in her socks.

The plate of cookies was sitting on the counter, next to the stove. Hilary looked at it strangely. There were no longer thirteen cookies. She counted quickly. Seven—no, eight. Someone had eaten five.

"Those twins!" she said aloud. But she knew it couldn't have been them. They never disobeyed, and their mother had said specifically that they could have no more. Besides, they had never left the sofa once the movie had started. And the only time she had left either one of them alone had been when she had taken Adam upstairs, leaving Andrew asleep . . . she stopped. Andrew hadn't been asleep. Not entirely. Still, she couldn't imagine Andrew polishing off five chocolate-chip cookies in the time it had taken her to tuck Adam into bed.

"Now . . ." she said to herself, "if it had been Dana Jankowitz!" She'd baby-sat Dana for almost a year before they moved away, and *that* kid was capable of anything.

Still puzzled, she went over to the plate of cookies, and as she got close, she stepped into something cold and wet. She looked down. There was a puddle on the floor, soaking into her right sock. An icy-cold puddle. Hilary looked out the kitchen window. It was raining.

*Someone was in the house.*

She didn't want to believe it, but there was no other explanation. Her whole body felt cold, and she could feel her heart stuttering in her chest. She thought about the twins sleeping upstairs; how she had told them she was hired to make sure nothing bad happened to them. But what if something bad happened to *her*? She shuddered and looked across the room. The telephone was hanging by the refrigerator. She could try and phone for help, or she could run outside and get to the nearest house. The Mitchells lived down a long driveway, and it was about a quarter mile to the next home. And dark. And wet. And she didn't know how many someones were in the house. Or outside. And maybe it was all her imagination.

But—and if her jaw trembled just the slightest she didn't think anyone could fault her—

what if the someones wanted to hurt the twins? She was the only one home to protect them.

As silently as possible, she slid open the knife drawer and took out a long, sharp carving knife. Then slowly she opened the door to the back stairs . . .

. . . and the man hiding there leaped at her. His face was hidden behind a gorilla mask. He was at least six feet tall, wearing blue jeans and a green shirt. She was so frightened, she dropped the knife and ran through the dining room, into the living room, and up the front stairs.

Calling, "Girly, girly, girly, come here," the man ran after her.

Hilary took the steps two at a time, shot around the corner, and ran down the hall. If only she could get to the twins' room, she thought, she could lock and barricade the door by pushing the dressers in front of it. And then she'd wake up the twins and they'd go through the trapdoor in the closet up to the attic. They'd be safe there.

But the man was pounding behind her, laughing oddly and calling out.

Hilary heard the chittering only after she passed the third door. And the man's screaming as she got to the twins' room. She didn't take time to look behind her, but slid into the room, slammed the door, rammed the bolt home, and slipped the desk chair under the doorknob. She didn't bother waking the twins or moving anything else in front of the door. The man's high screams had subsided to a low, horrifying moan. Then at last they stopped altogether. After all, he hadn't taken time to touch the doors or turn on his leg or kiss his fingers one at a time. He hadn't known the warding spell. *Once a night and you're . . .*

She waited a long time before opening the door and peeking out. When she did, all she could see was a crumpled gorilla mask, a piece out of a green shirt, and a dark stain on the floor that was rapidly disappearing, as if someone—or something—were licking it up.

Hilary closed the door quietly. She took a deep breath and lay down on top of the covers by Andrew's side. Next time she came to baby-sit, she wouldn't tell the "Golden Arm" story. Not next time or ever. After all, she owed *Them* a favor.

*Mark Garland has been, among other things, a school bus driver. This story is his revenge.*

# DEATH'S DOOR

## Mark A. Garland

Our regular driver was always giving speeches, though we barely listened anymore; over the years we'd heard them all a hundred times. That's how we knew he wouldn't be in on Friday. He'd given us the "Be good for the substitute" speech on Thursday. Of course, we could have done just that, but it would have spoiled our perfect record.

Bus 220 hadn't ever let a sub get through the whole run without turning him or her into a raving lunatic. We'd beaten them all. You spend half your life riding school buses, you get to be an expert.

We brought one poor woman to tears, and once we even sent some old guy running, screaming from the bus the instant we got to school. We had a reputation, and we'd earned it—along with a couple of hundred days' worth of detention, all combined. But that was the price you paid for being undefeated, for being the best: It was the price of fame.

Half the kids got on at the first stop so they could pick their seats. I usually got on at the second stop. Leonard always saved me a seat near the back. Leonard was thirteen, a year older than me, and much, much bigger. He was tough as they come. He didn't get in fights anymore because he'd punched out just about everyone worth fighting by the fifth grade. These days he was my friend, apprentice, and bodyguard. I had a reputation for being smart. Diabolically clever, actually. You know, a wise guy. A legend, sort of—which suited me fine.

I made Leonard laugh, along with everybody else—except Principal Miller, of course, who really didn't ever see the humor. Especially not the time we put sticky glue on the toilet seats in the faculty restroom. But that's another story. . . .

That Friday morning it was raining and still pretty dark, the way mornings are in early November. The bus pulled up and the door opened, and I saw the guy, the sub, sitting there, bone-thin and sickly looking, staring out the windshield. He wore black sneakers, black jeans, and a black, hooded sweatshirt with the sleeves pushed halfway up and the hood down. He had long black hair and black eyes and a tattoo on his right forearm that read: WE DELIVER.

Usually the drivers watch you getting on. Not his guy. I went down the aisle dispensing greetings and sat down next to Leonard, then pointed up front. "That guy's in a world of his own," I said.

Leonard grinned and nodded. "So what are we gonna do to him?"

The bus moved again, then stopped at the next corner. By the time we'd made all the stops, everybody was snickering about the driver and plotting, getting warmed up. The driver just stared straight ahead. He didn't even look up in the big mirror so he could see what we were doing.

I shook my head. "Talk about asking for it."

"This is going to be too easy," Leonard said.

The window next to our seat was one of those emergency exit types, with the long metal clamp across the bottom. I reached over in front of Leonard and pulled the clamp up. The buzzer sounded immediately, loud and annoying. It kept sounding for about a minute while the driver just drove, staring ahead. Until he stopped at a traffic light. He raised his right hand in the air. Suddenly the buzzer quit. He put his hand down. The bus was moving again.

I pushed the clamp shut, then popped it back open, then shut. The buzzer just wouldn't work.

Five seats from the front, a couple of Leonard's buddies, the Connery brothers, started fake fighting. The girls sitting across from them went along with the game, howling at the boys, picking favorites to win. Everybody on the bus started chanting, "Fight, fight, fight!"

Then one of the boys swung just as the bus hit a huge pothole—a hole I didn't remember being there. Anyway, he lurched and his fist hit the window and I heard it crack—his fist, I mean. He sat down and hugged his hand and started moaning like somebody had bitten it off. The driver just kept on staring straight ahead, kept driving.

"Hey, shut up!" somebody yelled at the Connery kid.

"You shut up!" both Connerys yelled back. Then everyone was doing it, yelling "SHUT UP!" or worse, at the top of their lungs. Which brought on the coughing attack.

Practically every kid on the bus seemed to be affected somehow. Just after the driver glanced over his shoulder, we all mysteriously started coughing and hacking and choking. It was as if we'd all come down with the flu at the same time. After a few minutes the fit passed. "This is weird," Leonard said. "We're having the worst luck."

"Or that guy leads a charmed life," I said, beginning to wonder. But I didn't think we were finished, not yet. I sat up and looked around. "Let's really get his attention," I announced. I tore a sheet of paper out of my notebook, held it up, and crumpled it in my fist. That was the signal, and it was followed by the ragged sound of paper being torn out of forty-six notebooks all at once. An instant later we opened fire.

Paper balls flew everywhere, bounced off everything, then got thrown again.

"Anybody hear anything on the news about a blizzard warning?" I shouted, and Leonard laughed out loud. A few balls of paper hit the driver in the back of the head. He raised his right hand again.

Suddenly all the flying papers burst into flames. They flashed white-hot and vanished, leaving only traces of ashes floating around inside the bus and the smell of smoke. I stared at the driver, waiting for some reaction, or maybe an explanation—anything! But he just kept looking straight ahead, hands on the wheel again.

No one dared move. We sat, frozen, not even blinking, as if we had been hypnotized. I realized I wasn't breathing and made myself

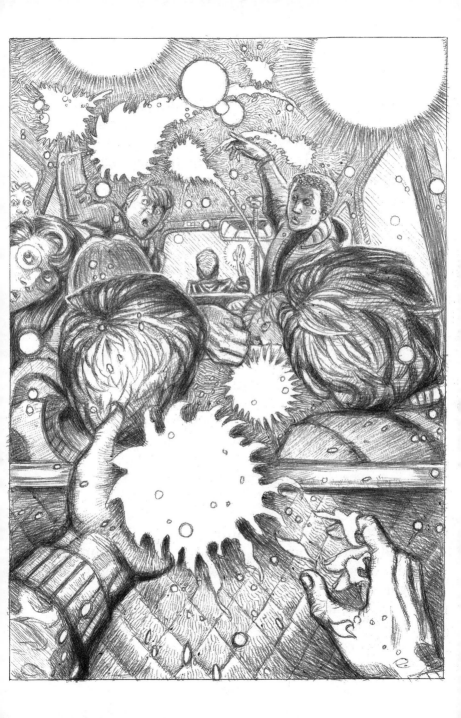

start again. That's when I looked past the driver, out the windshield, and decided something was very wrong.

It should have been bright daylight by now, and it wasn't. We weren't on the regular bus route anymore, either. We weren't anywhere in town at all.

I cleared my throat, took a deep breath, and cupped my hands. "Where are we?" I called to the driver.

No answer.

After a long time I asked again, and still got nothing.

"Helloooo!" somebody nearer the front sang out. The others were all breathing again, too, and they had begun to notice what I had noticed. They were busy wiping the steam off the insides of their windows, peering through the wet glass. Leonard seemed lost in concentration.

Everyone up front was trying to get the driver to say something now, though no one seemed eager to approach him. I waited as long as I could, then I swallowed hard. Somebody had to go. "Come on, Leonard," I said, figuring out who it would be. "You and I are going to get some answers."

"Right behind you," Leonard said, snapping out of his trance. We got up. Leonard's head nearly touched the ceiling. It made me feel better, knowing he was there. We moved up the aisle.

"You wanna tell us where we're going?" I asked the sub, standing right next to him. "We've got a right to know." I noticed he'd put the hood up on the sweatshirt. I could barely see his face, but the flesh almost looked like plain white bone.

"You have a date with destiny," the sub said in a low, straight, bone-chilling voice that would have made Darth Vader sound pretty cheerful. It made my heart pound.

"We have to get to school!" I told him. "Do you know what you're doing?"

"He's lost!" someone yelled.

"He's an idiot!" someone else added.

"You're gonna have a mutiny on your hands if you don't get this bus going the right direction," Leonard offered.

"It is headed in the right direction," the driver replied. "You've all been put in my capable hands. I have been sent to bring you in."

*He's nuts*, I thought. I was getting frustrated, so I decided to try a different approach. "You got a name?" I asked.

He nodded slowly.

I looked at Leonard. He just shrugged. I turned back to the driver. "Okay, so what is it?"

"Death."

I felt something turn hard in my stomach. "Death?"

The driver nodded, then pointed to the tattoo. "We deliver," he said.

I looked at Leonard again, who shrugged again. "I don't get it," he said.

"This bus is going to be in an accident, a terrible accident, and you are all going to die," Death explained. "It'll be such fun. For me, anyway. There's nothing you can do about it. These things happen, you see, and they are going to happen to you."

We hit a bump in the road. Without thinking, I put my hand on Death's shoulder to steady myself. My skin nearly froze before I could pull it away. I turned around and got behind Leonard, who seemed to be taking all of this rather lightly.

"Hey, Earth to Captain Zero!" Leonard jeered. He tried to get in Death's face. "You turn this thing around right now, or somebody might get hurt." The Connery brothers were getting up now, ready to back Leonard, more or less.

"Enough," Death said. He reached out, put his hand on Leonard's chest, and pushed. Leonard jerked back and slammed against the bus doors, then fell in a big, bent heap down in the stairwell. No one came to help. It took me a couple of minutes to get him up and out of there. He wouldn't stop moaning.

"Go back to your seats," Death said. "You'll be dead soon enough."

We went, and sat, and worried. I thought I heard some of the girls crying, but it turned out to be the Connery brothers. Death kept driving for a while, a very long while. Everybody talked in whispers. Right about the time I stopped shaking, I decided it was time to get a grip. "If we're going to die anyway, then we ought to try *something*," I suggested to anyone who would listen. "What have we got to lose?"

"You got any ideas?" Leonard asked, while several others leaned close all around.

"We've never seen a sub we couldn't beat. We're the experts! Maybe we aren't trying hard enough. I say we give it another shot."

"But he said there was nothing we could do," Leonard moaned. "He said this was our destiny!"

I was way ahead of him. "Yeah, but if we were on our regular route, with our regular driver, I think we'd be okay," I said, still working it out myself. "This Death guy is playing with the rules. Maybe he's gotta drive us somewhere strange to make our deaths happen."

Leonard made a sour face. "So we're not supposed to die?"

"Not unless we go his way—the wrong

**169**

way. Death is changing the odds. I figure we can do the same thing back."

Everybody was silent. "I still don't get it," Leonard said finally.

"Doesn't matter," I replied, standing up, getting people's attention, which is when I noticed how badly my legs were shaking. The driver continued staring straight ahead. "We give this guy the works," I said. "Starting right now!"

A feeble cheer swept the ranks. Within seconds, though, a new blizzard of papers was filling the air, every kid on the bus was screaming at maximum decibels, and half the kids had formed a team that lunged all together from one side of the bus to the other, trying to knock it over. I don't know who had the hard candy, but it was a nice touch. I thought the pieces that missed the driver were going to crack the windshield.

Just then the bus bounced a couple of times and stopped dead. Death pulled the keys out of the ignition and stood up. He turned and looked at us, took a spit ball in the forehead, then shook his head, grabbed the lever, and flung the door open. Next he held out his right hand and pointed to both of the emergency exit doors, the roof hatches, and all three emergency windows, including mine. Dark purple light glowed and crackled for an instant wherever he pointed.

I could see Death's face within the shadow cast by the hood of his sweatshirt. He was grinning now, thin white lips curling upward. I couldn't see his eyes. Suddenly he turned and leaped straight off the bus. The double doors slammed shut behind him.

Everybody applauded; they jumped up and down; they laughed like a bunch of first graders. I was too busy testing the clamp on my window. It wouldn't budge.

Then a girl up front tried to pull the main door open. She couldn't. "We're trapped!" the girl yelled. Everybody got worried all over again.

I took my sleeve and wiped more steam off the window. We were parked across a set of railroad tracks. Through the gloom I saw a bright headlight maybe a half mile away, then I heard the low moan of the whistle. A train was coming straight at us.

Everyone else had gotten the same idea about rubbing the windows. Somebody—it might have been me—yelled, "TRAIN!" After that everybody started to scream. A clump of kids were hanging on the main door lever, but it wouldn't budge.

"Fire drill!" one of the girls near me yelled, and people started tugging at the emergency doors and window hatch levers. Nothing opened.

Leonard grabbed me with both hands, finally losing it. "We're gonna die!" he wailed. "My mother is gonna kill me!"

"Wait!" I said, trying to think, trying to remind myself we were supposed to be experts. I vaguely remembered one of the regular driver's speeches, remembered just enough. "Leonard, come on!" I grabbed him by the shirt. We headed for the front, where I had him stand in the driver's seat. "Kick-out windshields!" I said. "Try one!"

Leonard stood staring a moment, then he nodded once and sat. He slouched down, braced himself against the seat back, planted both big feet on the glass, and heaved. The edge squeezed out, then the whole left half of the windshield popped free of the soft rubber moldings and bounced off the hood. Somebody in back caught on, and a second later they had the big window in the rear door pushed out.

I started climbing over the steering wheel behind Leonard, following him out onto the hood. The train was almost there. Our record was on the line. This was going to be close!

I stood on the side of the tracks and watched as the last kid bounded off the hood of the bus and sprinted toward the rest of us.

With a terrible crash the train barreled into the middle of the bus, bent it into a crumpled horseshoe, and booted it down the tracks like a kid kicking a loaf of bread.

I almost couldn't believe we'd made it.

Then I heard the laughter.

I turned around and there he was again: Death. He didn't look the least bit upset. He raised his hands toward the sky and held them apart. "Touchdown!" he said. "Well done!"

That was when I noticed that the sun still hadn't come up, and that, when I looked as far into the distance as I could, there *wasn't* any distance. The land, the sky, everything just seemed to fade into dark misty gray.

I was feeling ill. This wasn't over yet.

"Tomorrow," Death said with a grin, "we'll see how you do in the plane crash."

# ABOUT THE AUTHORS

ANNE MAZER lives in northeastern Pennsylvania with her family. She grew up in a family of writers in Syracuse, New York. Intending to be an artist, she studied at Syracuse University, then went to Paris for three years, where she studied French and French literature at the Sorbonne, and began to write. She is the author of three picture books, including *The Salamander Room*, and three novels, including *The Oxboy*, which was an ALA Notable Book. She has edited two anthologies: *America Street* and *Going Where I'm Coming From*.

DEBORAH MILLITELLO has been writing since she was in fourth grade and has had stories published in such magazines as *Marion Zimmer Bradley's Fantasy Magazine* and such anthologies as *Aladdin, Master of the Lamp*. This is her twelfth published story. She lives in southern Illinois, has three children, four grandchildren, and loves to read aloud to all of them.

JANNI LEE SIMNER grew up on Long Island and has been working her way slowly west ever since. She currently lives in Tucson, Arizona, and enjoys hiking in the mountains that surround the city. She's published over a dozen stories, including recent contributions to the young adult anthology *Starfarer's Dozen* and *Children's Playmate* magazine.

LAWRENCE WATT-EVANS is the author of about two dozen novels of science fiction, fantasy, and horror, and about five dozen short stories. "The Cat Came Back" is his third story in this series of anthologies. He lives in Maryland with his wife, two kids, two cats, a hamster, and a parakeet named Robin.

JOE R. LANSDALE is the author of a dozen novels, one young adult Batman novel, and well over one hundred short stories, many of them inspired by excessive popcorn consumption. Mr. Lansdale discovered that popcorn, a favorite snack of his, eaten before bedtime, causes him to have weird dreams—all of which, so far, have translated into strange stories. "The Fat Man" is an example.

EUGENE M. GAGLIANO shares his love of reading and writing with his second-grade class at Meadowlark School in Buffalo, Wyoming. He lives with his wife, Carol, and four children at the base of the majestic Big Horn Mountains.

MICHAEL MANSFIELD began teaching himself to make monster masks and elaborate costumes while he was still a kid. Later he went to Hollywood, where he worked as a robotics and special-effects wizard for movies—building sets, robot interiors, and monsters. He now designs math, science, art, and special-effects teaching programs for kids.

MICHAEL MARKIEWICZ teaches history in a private school for troubled teens. He lives in rural Pennsylvania with his wife and two "totally spastic" beagles. "Master of the Hunt" is the third in a series of stories featuring Cai and his brother, the future King Arthur. The other stories have been published in *Bruce Coville's Book of Monsters* and *Bruce Coville's Book of Ghosts*. Michael is currently working on a book about Arthur and his sharp-tongued brother.

MARY DOWNING HAHN is the author of the blood-chilling and extremely popular ghost story *Wait Till Helen Comes*, which won eleven state children's choice awards. A former children's librarian, she lives in Maryland with her husband, Norm (who is still a librarian), and a black cat named Holmes.

STEVEN PROHASKA was born in Kansas City, Kansas, and moved to Miami, Florida, at the age of four with his parents, Mark and Mai Prohaska, and his younger brother, James. He is an eighth grader at Hammocks Middle School and is a straight-A student in the gifted program. He has written everything from science fiction to fantasy adventure to scary stories. This is his second published story.

JANE YOLEN has published nearly a hundred and fifty books. Her work ranges from the slaphappy adventures of Commander Toad to such dark and serious stories as *The Devil's Arithmetic* to the space fantasy of her much beloved "Pit Dragon Trilogy." She lives in a huge old farmhouse in western Massachusetts with her husband, computer scientist David Stemple.

MARK A. GARLAND read a copy of Arthur Clarke's *The Sands of Mars* when he was twelve and proceeded to exhaust the local library's supply of science fiction. Eventually he tried writing short stories on his own, but got sidetracked into working as a rock musician and a race car driver. Finally he came back to science fiction and has published two novels and over two dozen short stories. Mark lives in Syracuse, New York, with his wife, their three children, and (of course) a cat.

JOHN PIERARD, illustrator, lives with his dogs in a dark house at the northernmost tip of Manhattan. *Bruce Coville's Book of Nightmares* is the fourth anthology he has illustrated in this series. His pictures can also be found in three of the books in the *My Teacher Is an Alien* quartet, in the popular *My Babysitter Is a Vampire* series, in the *Time Machine* books, and in *Isaac Asimov's Science Fiction Magazine.*

BRUCE COVILLE was born and raised in a rural area of central New York, where he spent his youth dodging cows and chores, and dreaming about going to other planets. He now lives in an old brick house in Syracuse, with his wife, illustrator Katherine Coville, and enough children and pets to keep life interesting. Though he has been a teacher, a toymaker, and a gravedigger, he prefers writing. His dozens of books for young readers include the bestselling *My Teacher Is an Alien* quartet, as well as the *Camp Haunted Hills* books, *Goblins in the Castle*, *Jennifer Murdley's Toad*, *Aliens Ate My Homework*, and *Jeremy Thatcher, Dragon Hatcher*.